Our Lady
of Black Diamond

BILL DODDS

All characters, names, and incidents
(except COVID-19) in this book
are entirely fictitious.
Well, God is real. And the Blessed Mother,
saints, and angels, but the author doesn't
think they'll sue him.
Perhaps give him a stern talking-to
down the road.

DEDICATION

To my dear son, Thomas

1

Debra Patrick stared out her bedroom window and growled. "Tomorrow morning," she said, "I want you to take a two-pound dump in their front yard."

No response.

"Arnold!" she shouted. "Do you hear me? I am talking to you."

Nothing.

Still not taking her eyes of the monstrosity next door, she yelled, "God *damn* it, Arnold!"

A grunt from the living room.

"What did I say?" she demanded.

Another grunt.

"Two pounds."

Sounds of a yawn.

"I don't know why I bother. You don't care. Don't tell me you care. You don't care."

The still-being-built house next door seemed to stare back at her. Not caring. As if to say, "So whatta you gonna do about it, old lady? Yeah. That's what I thought. Nothin'."

"Not nothing," Debra said to it. "Thirty-two ounces of not nothing."

She squinted.

"Daily."

She made a tight-lipped smile.

In thirty days, sixty pounds. One month.

Mid-February to mid-March. It was going to be a great spring.

"Who wants a treat?" she sang out and four paws clicked on hardwood flooring. Eighty pounds of mutt loped into the bedroom and a head the size of a basketball banged into the side of the Debra's leg.

"Well, look who can suddenly hear me," she said. "It's a miracle. Just what this house needs. A miracle."

Arnold ignored her as he ran to the kitchen and back. Twice. Then stopped and stared up at her, the look in his eyes saying, "Treat?" He butted his head into her leg again. He begged: *"Rurrr, rarrr, rurrr?"*

"Come on," Debra said and Arnold danced circles around her as she walked to the kitchen.

Three doggie biscuits and half a bowl of water later—two cookies and half a cup of coffee later—they sat side-by-side on the living room sofa, watching TV. More than side-by-side. Arnold's head rested in her lap.

"She has the better voice," Debra said nodding toward the screen. "but the other one has more zip. You need zip."

Arnold huffed.

"Well, *you* don't. A singer does. An entertainer. That first girl is kind of a limp wash rag. Pretty voice, though."

Arnold didn't disagree.

"You know what bothers me?" Debra asked. "You know what really gets my goat?"

Apparently, Arnold didn't.

"Thirty years. I've lived in this house for thirty years—three decades—and then ... ."

Then what? She thought for a moment.

"Then Amazon takes off and house prices in Seattle go

nuts and real estate agents and contractors starting sniffing around beyond Seattle, beyond the closer suburbs, and the next thing you know ... you know."

She scratched Arnold's ear and he showed his appreciation by shifting his shoulders a few times.

"What if they have a D-O-G?" she asked, spelling it so he wouldn't hear the word and run to the front window, ready to bark "hello," or "get away," or "I want to play."

"Some little, rat-sized D-O-G, some yapper. Millennials. Rich. A Tesla. Maybe two. Avocado on toast. That's a thing, right?"

Arnold stirred slightly at the word "toast."

"No toast." He looked up at her. She shook her head and he settled back down.

"What we're going to do," she said, "you and I are going to make sure nobody moves into that box house for a long, long time."

A plan. The beginning of a plan. Sixty pounds of poop.

Starting tomorrow.

2

The next morning it became apparent her idea was flawed. Arnold was set in his ways. *This* was where he went wee-wee and *that* was where he went poo-poo. And nothing in heaven or on earth was going change it.

Change him.

She should have known. She didn't blame him. At sixty-five, and having lived alone in her house since the late 1980s, she was set in her ways, too.

Dog nature. Human nature. Nature.

And now, in the cold, gray light of a Sunday morning, Debra knew throwing feces at a house in mid-construction wasn't going to stop its being completed.

Nothing was.

She'd throw in the towel but now holding more than half a pound of doggie doodie in a green, (supposedly eco-friendly plastic "pick up after your pet") bag, she might as well throw some of that, too.

A symbolic gesture. A way of saying: "I think this horrid shoe box looks like a giant outhouse."

"Pile of crap," she said and Arnold looked up at her. None of those words sounded like some form of food so he ignored her. Time to get back inside for a nap. The first of the morning.

They stood on the small, concrete front porch of her own house. "A home that looks like a home," she said, "not some shoebox set on its end."

It was a style gaining more and more popularity in Seattle. With those contractors, real estate agents, and young, pretty-much well-to-do Amazon techies and such. Buy a small lot, demolish a small house, and replace it with a three-story rectangular building. Huge square footage.

A shoe box. Gaining just about no popularity with the other folks on the block living in small houses on small lots. Zero aesthetics. That is: a shoebox sitting on one end. Tall. Slender.

Giving a neighborhood, here giving Debra, the finger in wood, metal, and glass.

She reached out and patted her front door. "*This* is a house that looks like a house."

Not too big, not too small. Two stories and a full basement. Two modest-sized bedrooms and a bath upstairs. Master bedroom with bath on the main floor. Living room, dining room, good-sized kitchen. Small bedroom and three-quarter bath in the basement.

Compact. Functional. Home.

"*This* is a house," Debra repeated as Arnold waited. Seemingly mesmerized by the chain-link fence across the front of the yard. Occasionally moving his head back and forth, keeping a keen eye on the asphalt road that had no curbs, no sidewalks.

A furry sentry.

No cars. No pedestrians. No squirrels.

All was well.

The dog looked up at Debra who had started to windmill her right arm clockwise, the green bag at the end of it extending from her hand.

Around and around.

And then, letting go.

And then, the bag rising, rising, rising.

And then, falling, falling, falling.

And then, a short Black woman, in a light brown car coat with some kind of a large dark brown scarf wrapped around her head so only her face showed, stepping out of the front doorway of the shoebox. Dark brown pants. Faded moon-gray running shoes. All items looking old and well-used.

Debra gasped and Arnold jumped up on his hind legs and leaned against the porch's wrought-iron railing, seeming to want a better view.

To not miss the show.

3

Time doesn't stand still. Time doesn't slow down.

Debra knew that. Everyone knows that. But on this morning, on this porch, as she watched that plastic weapon of mass defecation, it was like an old-fashioned slide show on a home projector.

Click.

Click.

Click.

Click.

Crap.

Right on top of the stranger's head.

The woman jumping, startled. The bag, unbroken, continuing its interrupted descent to earth. The woman touching the crown of her head. Looking up, wary of more, seeing none, looking around.

To her left.

To her right.

Bingo.

The two women staring at each other. Arnold giving a pleasant huff in greeting.

The woman raised her hand hello, misinterpreting Debra's

arm frozen at the top-of-the-windmill rotation.

Launch position.

It would be more than twenty-four hours later before Debra would think: *I should have pointed to my left, to the corner of the street, and said, "There they go! Did you see those two boys! I don't know who they are. They aren't from this neighborhood."*

Or some such.

Then and there, it would be more than a solid ten seconds before she would notice her arm, her hand, were pointing toward the sky.

She slowly brought them down to her side. She slowly dropped her chin to her chest. It was an I-want-the-earth-to-open-up-and-swallow-me moment.

That dragged on and on.

Then the woman said something. Not shouting, not yelling, not screaming, but loud enough for Debra and Arnold to hear her.

They both looked at her, the woman now holding the bag in her right hand.

At least it hadn't split open, Debra thought.

Now the woman was repeating what she had said. "A new translation of Matthew 5:45: 'he maketh the poop to fall on the just and the unjust.'"

She smiled, tossed the bag into a large metal trash bin a dozen feet from the house's doorway, and headed for the chain-link fence that separated Debra's lot from her neighbor's.

Her neighbor's? It had been an empty, corner, odd-shaped, tiny, scrub-tree-riddled, and blackberry-bush-infested piece of land for ... well, forever. At least in her time. Debra was sure of that.

Now Arnold and the woman were at the fence but Debra seemed unable to move.

Now the woman was bending over the top of the fence and Arnold was on his hind legs and leaning in to smell the lady's scarf and hair.

Something familiar ... .

Now the woman was laughing as Arnold licked her face.

Debra moved her right foot. One step down. Then another and another and another until she was on the lawn and moving toward the fence.

"Miriam," the woman said. "Or Maryam." Debra nodded, having no idea what she was talking about.

The woman held the dog's head in her hands and gently shook it back and forth. "And this is ... ?"

"Arnold," Debra said, her voice sounding not-right.

"Hello, Arnold! Who's a good boy, huh? Whoooosa good boy?"

She looked up. "And you're?"

"Uh, Debra."

"Hello, Debra. Say, could you spare a cup of coffee?"

"Uh, sure."

4

Lawsuit, Debra thought. *Be nice, get her to say she isn't injured. Record it? How?*

She slipped her hand into her right coat pocket, pulled out her phone and ... what? Yes. Pretended to check for messages, tapped the record app, tapped record.

Both women were heading for Debra's front gate. Both women and Arnold. He oh-so excited to have company. Debra far less than thrilled.

She opened the gate and held out her hand. Miriam took it in both of hers.

"My goodness," Debra said, "are you all right. After the ... incident?

Miriam looked a little confused. "Oh, yes. Right as rain. No harm, no foul."

"You weren't hurt?" That last word more swallowed than spoken so maybe the phone didn't catch it. "You weren't hurt?" she said, a little louder than necessary, unless one wanted a very clear legal ... something.

Was recording legal? Without the permission of all parties? Debra had watched a lot of cop and courtroom shows so she had her doubts. On the other hand, this woman looked suspicious.

Not that I'm racist but she's not a neighbor. Plus what was she doing in the half-built house? A squatter? Homeless? A thief? A danger? Should I take back the coffee offer, go inside, and call someone? If you see something …

The woman could say something: "That lady assaulted me with a bag of dog poop."

Poop.

"Please come in," Debra said but didn't move.

For all I know she's the new owner of the weird-shaped lot and it's her house or a house for her son or daughter. And the kids. And a dog. Or dogs. And cousins. Multigenerational, extended-family.

"Poop," she said. Out loud!

Poop!

"Are you all right?" the woman asked. "Do you need help? Can I do something?"

What a con artist! The long con. The big score. All the pieces fit except for the fact I'm lower-middle class.

"I'm fine," she lied. "Come inside."

"No, really. It was lovely to meet you and Arnold, even under such unusual circumstances." She laughed. A good laugh. Much louder and more hearty than one would expect from such a small person.

Maybe four inches less than Debra's five-five. Maybe ten, okay twenty, all right!, thirty pounds less than Debra's one … something. About the same age. Mid-sixties. Again, all right!, a couple years younger.

The tiny visitor laugh-snorted. Arnold barked and ran around her. Once. "Oh, excuse me," she said to the dog. Another bark. Another circle.

"Are you from this area?" Debra asked, now that the woman seemed loosened up.

Foreigner!

"Just visiting."

"Staying long?"

"A while I guess." She shrugged.

"Do you own the land or house next door?" This with a little nod to the construction.

"What? No," she said, looking a little guilty. Then in a whisper: "I was just snooping."

"So you're not going to sue me for beaning you with a bag of doggy doody."

"Sue you?" she said. "No, no, no. Oh, you Americans!"

Uh oh.

5

Be cool, Debra. Take your time. Wait for your moment.

Coats—and scarf (*or whatever it's called*)—were off, coffee was made, bread was toasted, butter and marmalade were put out on the kitchen table and still … the moment had yet to arrive.

Arnold, having inhaled two slices, content on the floor at their feet.

Debra was unclear what that moment would be but she was sure she'd know it when it came along. Any moment now could be *the* moment. And then, then she'd do a little low-key interrogating and get some big-time answers.

"Did I hit her in the head with a bag of dog poop? Is that what she's saying, officer?

No. *"Is that what she's saying, agent?"* Yeah. *FBI. Federal offense. Or Homeland Security. Were they officers or agents?*

No matter. Debra would be ready.

"Why that's ridiculous! Why on earth would I do that? That's just silly. How could anyone hit another person in the top of the head with a bag of dog poop? I was on the my front porch when I saw her come out of that building site next door."

"Building site." That sounded good.

Did she need more? Probably not. Not necessary to toss in the woman was saying "slalom alick 'em" or some such. To fudge the truth.

Oh, my God! I said on the tape that I hit her in the head. On the recording. Whatever.

She picked up her nearby cell phone. Tap, tap, delete.

"Ooh," her breakfast guest said.

Both of them sitting at the table.

"Huh?"

"I just bit into a nice-sized chunk of orange peel. This is so good! Everything is. The coffee, the toast, the butter, the jam. I mean marmalade."

"Real butter," Debra said, unable to help herself.

"Makes such a difference," the woman said.

"I'm sorry," Debra said. "I have something to confess."

Her guest said nothing.

"I have completely forgotten your name," Debra said. Which, in fact she had.

"Miriam," the woman said and patted her lips with a paper napkin.

"Miriam. Such a pretty name. Why, I don't think I've ever met a Miriam."

"Well, I hope I'm a good representative."

Debra gave a hollow laugh and nodded a little too vigorously. "I don't know about the others, but you're quite lovely."

Again, the truth.

"You're very kind," Miriam said.

"And you don't have any accent." *Hell, hell, hell! Why had she said that? It was true, too, but why had she said it?*

Miriam leaned in a little. "I do," she whispered and Debra leaned back a little. "But it's just like yours," Miriam said."

"Mine?" Clearly confused.

"Yes. Everyone has an accent. Yours and mine are mainstream American English."

Oh. She had never thought of that. It was always just her

14

and everyone who didn't pronounce words the way she did. That is, people with accents. Who mispronounced words.

Inspiration! The moment had arrived. Welcome, welcome, welcome.

"My full name is Debra Therese Patrick," she said. "What's yours."

"Oh, Miriam is pretty much it. Different versions in different languages but all meaning the same."

"Huh?"

"Like 'Debra,'" she said. "Or Deborah. Both coming from the same source. Originally. Meaning bee. Like a honey bee."

Debra was pleased. She'd always admired hard-working honeybees. The idea of being a queen bee had never entered her mind.

"And 'Miriam,'" Debra said. "What does that mean?"

"Oh, several different things."

Back to it! Grilling her. For the feds.

"And what are your middle and last names?"

"It's just Miriam. Or one of the other translations."

That was disappointing.

"So," Debra said, "Like Cher or ... " *Who was that new one?* "Beyond-Say."

"Kind of like that," Miriam said.

"Or ... " Debra on a roll here. " ... like Madonna."

Miriam had just taken a sip of coffee that was still in her mouth. She looked like her face might explode with so much laughter trapped behind clamped teeth and lips.

The coffee escaped through her nose. Then the laughter, through her mouth.

A snort. A sniff. A cough. Another cough. Another cough.

Arnold stood, investigating.

Miriam covered her mouth and nose with her napkin but managed to say, "Went down the wrong pipe." A few shallower coughs. "Yes, like Madonna."

Then the dog's head hit the floor with the sound of dropped bowling ball.

6

"Thank you," Debra said from the back seat of the car. Arnold splayed out next to her. Breathing. Eyes open. "Could you go a little faster."

"Of course," Miriam said, seemingly still more than a bit surprised that Debra had taken her up on her offer to do the driving.

It was twenty minutes since the dog had had a stroke or a seizure or passed out. Ten more to the vet, who was expecting him.

"Erin said it's probably nothing serious," Debra repeated for the second time.

"Probably not," Miriam agreed.

"I think he looks a little more perky. Less loopy."

"Cookie!" Miriam shouted without turning around and Arnold moved his head a little her way.

"Probably nothing serious," Debra said.

"Probably not."

"And thanks for helping me get him in the car," Debra said. "I don't know what I would have done without you."

"Here to help," Miriam said. "Glad to. And you know what? It's probably nothing serious."

"You think?"

"I do."

Then the conversation turned to street directions. Given in the back, repeated in the front. Minutes later they pulled up at the vet's and some young, and very strong, assistants came out to the car and put Arnold on some kind of wheeled cart.

A doggy gurney.

Debra followed it into an exam room and Miriam took a seat in the lobby. Or "waiting room." Either way, it had comfortable chairs and more than enough magazines about all kinds of pets.

She leafed through them for forty-five minutes until Debra's happy voice interrupted her.

"Doctor Erin was right," Debra said, plopping down in the chair beside Miriam. "I was right. You were right. We all were right. She said it wasn't serious."

"Oh, that's wonderful."

"But she wants to keep him overnight and do a few more tests. Just to be on the safe side."

"The best side to be on," Miriam said.

"Oh, my!" Debra said. Relief clearly on her face. She exhaled loudly. "Oh, my."

"Home tomorrow," Miriam said.

"Home tomorrow. Will you stay with me?"

"What?"

"Tonight. Will you stay with me?"

"Would you like me to?"

"Oh, please," Debra said.

"Of course."

"The house is just too big and too quiet without Arnold."

"Quite a difference." Miriam said.

"I don't know why I bought such a big one."

Forgetting that just earlier that morning she had considered it midsized.

"No, I do know," she went on. "I bought it because it was

17

a good deal."

Miriam let her ramble. Adrenaline.

"Did I tell you I hate the shoebox house they're putting up next door?" Debra asked.

"It's a different style, all right."

"It's got *no* style. Three stories and a big blank wall ten feet from my bedroom and living room windows. On the east. Goodbye pretty sunrises." She took a deep breath and changed the subject. "I hate to impose."

"No imposition at all. Really. There's nowhere else on earth I'd rather be."

"You are just so sweet," Debra said and tapped her on the knee.

"Like orange marmalade," Miriam said.

Then more to herself than to her visitor: "And to think I was afraid you were some kind of terrorist."

Laugh. Snort. Laugh.

7

Nearly midnight and Debra still couldn't fall asleep. She lay in bed, tired and wired.

Tired from the day's event. Wired from worrying about Arnold. Yes, he was in good hands. Yes, it wasn't anything serious. The overnight stay was only a precaution. But why was a precaution necessary if it wasn't anything serious?

But it wasn't. She had almost convinced herself that it really wasn't when the cost of the testing and overnight stay popped into her head. She hadn't thought to ask what both would add up to. They hadn't said.

Well ... .

Worst of all Arnold wasn't here on top of the covers. Sleeping peacefully and claiming more and more of the bed as the night progressed.

And then there was some woman in the basement. Miriam. Yes, she seemed nice enough—very nice, really—but one never knows. One can't be sure.

Oh, but certainly it was all right offering her the bedroom down there. Just for tonight.

Ha! Finally an overnight guest in the house and Debra hadn't even offered her "the guest room." One of the bedrooms upstairs. The first crammed with a single bed, assorted odd bits of furniture, boxes, and clothes. The second her "sewing room." Not that she had sewn anything for a while.

A while. Might have been a decade.

That room stuffed with a single bed, fabric, patterns, and countless half-finished projects.

But tomorrow, or later today really, she would pick up Arnold, drive Miriam to the airport or bus station or wherever it was she had been heading, and that would be that.

Just the two of them again. She and her best friend.

"Damn it, Arnold," she said out loud and it made her smile.

When did the vet's open? They'd take a credit card. It would be okay.

How much? A hundred? No, more than that. A thousand? Oh, dear God. No, not that much. Maybe two hundred. Not good but not bad. Not really bad.

Why had she taken her Social Security benefits last year at age sixty-five? Why hadn't she waited until she was seventy?

"Because you needed it," she said.

This, this wasn't how she had seen her life unfolding. Once a young married woman with a daughter and then …

She sighed. How many times had she been over this in her head?

A little family and then booze and then some drugs and then some "boyfriends" and then a divorce and then her ex-husband with complete custody of their seven-year-old.

Even then, still the booze, the drugs, the men.

"Don't beat yourself up," she said.

Then ending up on the other side of the country. Staying completely out of their lives. Her life. Emily's. It was for the best.

The tears came.

They always did.

8

Thumping, Pounding. Grinding. Dropping Yelling. Seven-thirty in the morning.

"You hear that?" Debra asked and got no response. It took her a moment to remember yesterday. Arnold wasn't on the bed. Or in the bed.

The shoe box house. The workers. Her ruined view. Her ruined neighborhood.

Coffee. She smelled coffee.

Miriam

Oh God, Miriam.

Okay. Get Arnold, get rid of her and … . That was enough for one day. That would make it a good day.

Twenty minutes later she walked into the kitchen and found Miriam ready to make waffles.

"I hope you don't mind," she said, handing Debra a cup of coffee. "I found the mix in the cupboard and had noticed the waffle iron on a shelf in the basement and … " She shrugged.

"Oh. No that's … There was mix in the cupboard?"

"And the best-by date was still good."

Debra wondered how long a box of mix lasted on a shelf. When had she bought one? Why? She had forgotten all about the waffle iron.

"I don't know if it works," she said.

"Heated up okay," Miriam said. "Shall we live dangerously?"

"I don't know if I have any … "

"Found this, too." A bottle of syrup. Unopened.

"Well, great. Thank you."

"Oh, I like cooking," Miriam said. "I always loved doing it for … " She stopped abruptly. "A while back."

Aha!

Divorce? Death? Drugs? Abandonment? Ungrateful husband or kids? All of the above?

"This is a real treat," Debra said. "I can't remember the last time someone made breakfast for me. Homemade."

They chatted about their favorite restaurants and fast-food menu items as Miriam made the first waffle. She tried insisting that Debra begin eating but got nowhere. Same with trying the give Debra the hot one when the second waffle was done.

"Please," Miriam said, "let me do this."

They each had one more and seriously considered splitting a final one. Then decided to save it for Arnold if the vet said it was okay.

"Remind me to ask her," Debra said, surprised to find herself wanting Miriam to go with her.

"Of course." Then looking serious. "There's something I want to talk to you about."

Here it comes.

"I'd like to stay here three more nights instead of going to a motel," she said. "I'll stay out of your hair." She reached into her pants pocket and pulled out some cash. "And here. It would cost me at least this much at a motel."

It looked like a lot of money, but Debra hadn't been to a motel for a long time. She had no idea how much a room cost in 2020. She picked up the cash and fanned it with the ball of her thumb and side of her index finger.

All fifties! No ones or fives.

"I can't possibly take … "

"I'd much rather you have it than some motel chain. And, you never know when you might need a little extra cash."

Arnold. Vet. Exam. Tests. Overnight stay.

"I guess that would be okay," Debra said. Thank you."

"No, thank *you!*"

9

The receptionist gave a chipper "Good morning!" when they walked through the front door at 9:15. Debra assumed her tone meant Arnold was doing fine

"Good morning. How's ... "

"Great. Ready to get back home with his family."

Debra sagged a little and Miriam reached forward to help her.

"Have a seat and Doctor Erin will be out in just a few minutes," the receptionist said.

"And Arnold is ... "

"Ate, peed, pooped. Bouncing all around."

"I think I hear him," Debra said, noticing some barking back in the examination rooms and kennel. A lot of barking by more than one dog.

"You hear that?" Debra asked Miriam. "There! That! HI, ARNOLD!"

One particular barker got louder.

"We could sit over ... " Miriam begin.

"Oh, I can't sit. I'm too jumpy. Like a kid on Christmas morning."

"A kid on Christmas morning," Miriam said and smiled.

The door to the back opened and Arnold shot out, abruptly stopped, looked left-right-left-right, and leaped at Debra. She dropped to one knee, he stood on his hind legs and put his front paws over her shoulders.

They hugged. They kissed. They made all kinds of happy sounds. The vet, the receptionist, and Miriam watched.

Then: "As you can see, he's fine" Erin said. "We could do a lot more testing and then we might be able to narrow down why he ... "

"No more testing," Debra said. "Does he need more testing?" A thread of worry in her voice.

"No. How about if we put this down to 'cause unknown' and assume it was a one-time event?"

"And that's okay to do?"

"Absolutely. Any concerns later on, you just get back in touch with us."

Debra hopped up and hugged the vet. Arnold ran in circles around them, and Miriam eased over to the receptionist counter.

She placed some cash on it. "Will this be enough?" she said softly.

"Let's see," the receptionist whispered. She checked her computer, counted the cash, and said, "Close. Short by twenty-one ... "

The vet gave a little cough, the receptionist looked her way, and the vet slightly shook her head one time. The young woman behind the counter quietly said, "Paid in full. I'll get you your receipt."

Arnold went from four legs to three and urinated on a large potted plant in the corner. Watering some kind of ficus.

10

The drive home from the vet was infinitely cheerier than the previous day's drive to the vet had been.

Miriam in the front passenger seat, Arnold in the back leaning over into the front and licking Debra's right ear. Debra, driving and singing "There was a lady had a dog and Arnold was his name-o ... "

"Would you mind stopping at a grocery store?" Miriam asked.

"Sure. Happy to."

Happy to do anything because Arnold was all right and on his way home. Their home.

She pulled into a supermarket parking lot, parked the car, shut off the engine, and said, "Take your time. "We're fine."

"Thank you," Miriam said, getting out and heading to the store's nearest entrance.

Arnold lay down on the back seat. Debra reclined the driver's seat. Both closed their eyes and someone gently tapped on the driver's window.

Miriam.

With a full paper shopping bag in her arms. Obviously heavy. "I guess I went a little wild," she said.

"What?" Debra lowered her window.

"I said I guess I went a little wild."

"Okay." She popped the trunk.

Whatever.

Back home Arnold made a quick but thorough sniff-tour of the front yard and, once inside, of every room with an open door.

Miriam set the sack of groceries on the kitchen table and started unpacking it. A variety. Some treats Debra seldom bought for herself. Treats she *really* liked, but too expensive.

Some "Arnold treats," too.

"Funny what you learn from your mother," Miriam said. "I mean Mama was always huge on returning hospitality. When someone takes you into their home you don't come emptyhanded."

"But why," Debra said and gestured at all the … stuff, "why so many and so much?"

Miriam shrugged. "Oh, you never know."

"I don't mean to pry," Debra said, "but can you afford all this? I mean, the way you're dressed and, I don't know, you don't come off as stinking rich or anything."

"It's so sweet you're concerned," Miriam said, "but I'm fine."

"Uh huh. Are you on, you know, medication? Nothing wrong with that. If it helps, great, take it."

Miriam shook her head.

"Or not taking something you *should* be taking?"

Another shake.

Debra pressed. "Women our age, you know, early sixties, it's pretty common we need this or that for body or, uh, mind."

"That's true," Miriam said.

Probably walked away from a … facility

"Is there someplace you're supposed to be?" Debra gently asked.

Miriam nodded. "Here," she said.

"So ... no meds?"

"I'm blessed."

11

Twenty-four hours later, Debra stood alone in the kitchen, left hand white-knuckle gripping the landline extension phone's receiver held against her ear.

Mouth hanging open.

As with many ... seniors ... Debra had unconsciously begun setting price points for countless items. A gallon of milk. A pound of hamburger. A movie ticket. And on and on. *This* is what that *had* cost back whenever and now it's *how much!*

She had called the vet to ask about the bill for Arnold's treatment and boarding and had just been told the amount by that perky receptionist. A lot more than she had expected. Dreaded.

Then the young woman (whom Debra had begun to think of as "Perky") said: "No, wait, ma'am. Let me just ... Here it is. That's what I thought. Yep, you're all paid up."

So, wrong about the cost and the payment. Or maybe right on payment but as long as it wasn't *her* bill she didn't care about that.

"So how much do *I* ... "

"I remember," Perky said. "Your friend paid it."

"My 'friend'?"

"The other lady." Perky perhaps half swallowing "old" between "other" and "lady."

"My dog is Arnold."

"Right. Paid in full."

"When ... "

"You were talking to, well, hugging, Doctor Erin."

She thought about that. "Do you mail me a receipt or am I ... "

"Your friend has it."

Silence.

"So," Perky said, "is there anything else we can do for you today?"

"Uh, no. Uh, thanks."

"No problem. You and Arnold have a great day."

"Uh huh"

"Buh bye."

"Uh huh."

What in the hell?

Sure money was tight but she wasn't some charity case. Money for staying three nights. Two more to go. Money for the vet bill. Groceries.

What in the hell?

She walked to the basement door and hollered down the stairs. "Miriam?"

"Hello."

"Can we talk for a minute?"

"Sure. Be right there."

In less than thirty seconds: "So, what's up?" Miriam asked. Both woman standing in the kitchen.

Debra wasn't sure where, or how, to begin.

"I was thinking I'd make some bread today," Miriam said. "It's been a while since I did that."

An opening!

"Oh?" Debra said. "When was the last time?"

"Years."

"And where was that?"

"Let me think. I can see the kitchen. One of those brick, well, stone ovens. Like a pizza oven. Sort of burns the edges, but in a good way."

"I called the vet's." Debra blurted, "and they said you paid the bill for Arnold's treatment and overnight stay."

"Oh. Shoot. I forgot." She reached into her front pants pocket and pulled out a folded sheet of paper. "For your records."

Debra took it, looked at it, and sighed. "Why, in the name of heaven, would you ... ?"

"You and that dear mutt were having such a good time I just figured I could get this out of the way. On me."

"I found the grocery store receipt in the bottom of a bag," Debra said.

"Uh huh."

"And I added up what you gave me to stay here three nights, what the vet bill was, and how much you spent at the grocery store."

"Uh huh."

"Are you *nuts!*"

Apparently the time for beating around the bush was gone.

"Oh ... ."

"Yeah. Oh."

12

"How to put this?" Miriam said and paused. "I have, my life has been, I'm able to, part of my vocation now … ."

Debra waited.

"Don't be afraid," Miriam said.

"Afraid?"

"I have to say that a lot."

"What's 'a lot'?"

Miriam shrugged.

"Okay," Debra said, "why do you have to say it?"

"Sometimes people are afraid."

"Of you?"

"Well, yes. And of what's happening to them."

"So," Debra said, "you don't want me to be afraid of what's happening to me."

"Right." Miriam looked pleased.

"And what's happening to me?"

"I'm here," Miriam said.

"Uh huh.

"And some things I do can be … unsettling."

"'Unsettling.'"

"Right."

"Uh huh," Debra said again.

"Like being a little loose with money," Miriam said.

"That's not normal."

"Right."

"So why do you do it? Why *did* you do it?"

"You needed help and I could help you."

"And you're leaving the day after tomorrow. Two more nights here."

"If you like."

"And," Debra said, "you would leave right now if I told you to."

"Yes."

"And I could keep all the money."

"Of course. It's yours."

"So what's your deal?" Debra said.

"'My deal'?"

"Yeah."

"No one has ever asked me that … in that way."

"There's always a first for everything," Debra said.

So just pack up your stuff and …

"Why don't you have any stuff?" Debra asked.

Miriam looked as if she didn't understand.

"Bag. Backpack. Suitcase. Toiletries. Changes of clothes. Stuff!"

"I don't need stuff."

"Everybody needs stuff," Debra said, with more than a little heat in her voice.

"That's true, that's true. But not after they die. You know: 'You can't take it with you.'"

What was the word? Exis … something. Existent … Existentialism. Wow! Pulled that one out of my … Life, death, and crap like that.

"How about if we sit down?" Miriam said, pointing at the kitchen table.

Debra sighed. "Sure, why not?"

Each woman pulled out a chair and sat. "Is it okay if I give

Arnold a dog biscuit?" Miriam asked.

Arnold. Debra had forgotten about Arnold, at their feet the whole time. Perhaps turning his head left and right like someone watching a tennis match.

"Sure," Debra said.

"The waffle first?" Yesterday morning's leftover.

"Sure." Then: "Well, let's just get right to it. Are you dead? Did you die? Yes or no?"

"That's ... complicated."

"Oh, dear Lord." Debra folded her arms, put them on the table, and laid her forehead on them. "Go ahead," she mumbled.

"Some people believe I never died but was just taken up to heaven."

"Uh huh," in a muffled voice.

"Others say I did die but came back to life and was taken up to heaven."

"Uh huh."

"Sort of potato/potahto."

"Uh huh."

"One fellow just wrote 'having completed the course of her earthly life.'"

"'Completed the course of *her* earthly life' ... No! At the end of *your* earthly life, what?"

"I was taken up to heaven."

"Well, good for you."

"Oh, yeah."

"You just flew up to heaven."

"No, I was assumed into heaven."

"Well, you know what they say. To assume makes an ass of ... Wait a second."

This lady is cuckoo.

All roads led to it.

But.

Debra lifted her head, uncrossed her arms, and put her palms on the table.

The faint stirrings of a childhood memory.

Catholic stuff.

"You … you think …you think you were assumed into heaven so you, what?, you think you're the Virgin Mary?"

Miriam spread her arms forward, inviting a hug.

"Tada!"

13

"Prove it."

"Ooh, this is the fun part," Miriam said, rubbing her hands together.

"Yeah, well, do some magic trick."

"I don't do magic."

"Excuse me," Debra said. "Do a miracle."

"I don't do miracles."

"I'm pretty sure I was taught you do miracles. Healings and stuff."

"Stuff like water into wine?"

"Sure, that'll do," Debra said. "Make it a chardonnay."

"I've never done water into wine. That was Little Jay."

"'Little Jay'?"

"Yes. At a wedding reception. I just pointed out to him that the wine was running low."

"'Little Jay'?"

"Yes."

"And is there a 'Big Jay'?"

"Yes."

"Uh huh," Debra said. "And that would be ... who? Jehovah?"

"Ooh, very good. Really. That never occurred to me but

no. Yes and no. Yes, certainly could be but, no, that's not what … "

"Okay, Miriam, then who … No, wait. I though your name was Mary."

"In English."

"And it's 'Miriam' in … ?"

"Hebrew."

"You're Jewish."

"Of course."

"Of course," Debra said.

"And Little Jay's first follower. I followed him all over the place once he started to crawl. And when he started to walk!"

Nothing.

"That's a joke," Miriam said.

"A joking Virgin Mary."

"Everybody likes joking around."

"Even God?" Debra asked, determined to trip up her strange guest and then get her out of there.

"Oh, yes. He invented humor. Created it. Made all of us in his image. A good laugh pleases him."

"So Little Jay … I got it. Big Jay is Joseph."

"Right."

"And Big Jay was funny?" Debra asked.

"One of the many reasons I loved him."

"For instance."

"Let's see. Right after Little Jay was born and we were in that barn-stable-cave thing, Big Jay knelt beside me and the baby and said, "I was a little worried it would be twins.""

No reaction from Debra.

""Two girls," Miriam said. Then staring off into the distance and smiling a little smile.

Nothing from Debra.

"Okay," the houseguest said. "Little Jay is about five and 'helping' Big Jay in the shop and Little Jay gets a tiny bit of sawdust in his eye. And does he howl!"

"Jesus howled."

"He was a kid. Of course he howled."

"Uh huh. And … ?"

"And Big Jay gets Little Jay's eye cleaned up and then he picks up this plank and puts the end of it near his own eye and yells, 'Ow, ow, ow, now this *really* hurts!'"

Still nothing from Debra.

"I guess you had to be there," Miriam said, sounding a little disappointed.

"I guess."

"You want to hear how we had to sell the gold, frankincense, and myrrh to cover our travel expenses to Egypt?"

"No. I want a miracle but you don't do miracles."

"But I can ask Little Jay. He's a good son."

"Fine."

"But it can't be like some 'I want my first of three wishes to be that all my wishes come true.'"

"It seems there are a lot of rules to this," Debra said.

"No-o-o-o. Not rules. Just, the way it is."

Debra thought about that. "Uh huh. Then heal Mrs. McConkey. I mean, ask Jesus to heal Mrs. McConkey."

"Very nice. Really. Very nice. Praying for someone else. Who is Mrs. McConkey and what's her ailment?"

"Oh, no. I've got my own rules. Jesus knows who she is and what her troubles are, right? So just tell him to take care of it."

"Ask him to take care of it."

"Yeah, 'ask him.'"

"Okay."

She reached forward and took Debra's hands in hers.

14

"You're kidding," Debra said, pulling her hands free.

"Sorry," Miriam said.

"You just, you just do it."

"Okay."

"Out loud."

"Okay."

"In English."

"Sure." She smiled. "I'm multilingual."

"Well, pin a rose on you."

"Or put a crown on my head," Miriam said and Debra blushed.

"Look," Debra said. "I'm sorry about the bag of dog sh … poop but I didn't … "

"Oh, no," Miriam said. "That was hi*la*rious! You never heard three archangels laugh so hard. No, I mean second grade. At St. Augustine's. Mrs. Machnick's class. May Day. You put a crown of little plastic roses on a statue of me. On my head."

A speechless Debra violently pushed her chair back from the table, bumping into Arnold who yelped and bolted.

"Here we go," Miriam said. "Here we go. Be not afraid."

Debra felt her heart racing.

"Little Jay," Miriam said, eyes closed, "if it's the Father's will, please help Mrs. McConkey."

"Amen," Debra whispered. Involuntarily. Then: "You've been watching me?"

"You mean like stalking?" Miriam asked. "Oh, no. Nothing like that. It's just that when you talk to me I listen to you."

"Back then I was talking to you?"

"Oh, that little girl had a pretty voice singing a pretty song."

Silence.

"'O Mary, we crown thee with blossoms today'?" Debra said.

"Uh huh."

"You heard that?"

"Well, sure."

"But ... . But ... ."

"And now," Miriam said, " we get into 'So just how does all this work?'"

Silence. Then Debra nodded. "Yeah. That."

"I could tell you," Miriam said, "but then I'd have to kill you."

"What!"

"Oh, come on, Debra. An old joke. One I've wanted to use for quite a while and I thought you were a person who would appreciate it. But now I see ... not under these circumstances."

"You're creeping me out."

"Sorry."

A revelation. "Oh, fu ...udge," Debra said. You're not nuts because you're not really here. I'm talking to myself. I'm nuts. Excuse me. Have mental health issues."

"God bless those who do."

Silence.

"I have so many questions," Debra said.

"I know."

"You're reading my mind!"

"No, no, no," Miriam said. "I just meant this ain't my first rodeo."

"There! That! The Virgin Mary wouldn't talk like that."

Silence.

"Would she?" Debra asked, leaning forward and looking at this small, attractive, Black woman more closely.

"I like to dress and speak appropriately. Look appropriate. In step with the times. The place. The person."

Silence.

"This is my 'Debra Patrick' ensemble," Miriam said, waving her hand up and down in front of herself. "Early twenty-first century for the woman in her early sixties."

Silence. Then from Debra: "Mid."

"Now," Miriam said, "really. What can I do for you?"

Silence.

"How about if I top up that cup of coffee?" she asked.

Silence.

"And bake cookies," Miriam added.

Arnold blew back into the room. Sniffing for cookies.

Debra was motionless.

15

A little later Miriam went to work on a batch of snickerdoodles, Debra went for a walk, and Arnold stayed home and went a little wild anticipating whatever was being cooked, baked, or fried.

After a brisk mile Debra slowed her pace, took several deep breaths, and stopped.

She'd gone back to being almost completely certain she had lost her mind. And, since it was her mind, *that* was how her imaginary visitor knew about the statue-crowning in second grade. Even if she, Debra, had forgotten about it.

Stress.

That was the problem. There was more news of some spreading flu or some such. A virus. Taken the lives of some old people, really old people not mid-sixties, up in a Kirkland nursing home. Or whatever it was called.

Up east of Seattle.

So there was that plus the stupid house being built next door—practically touching her house.

The combination has had … .

What?

Given her this bizarre dream.

Of course.

She was probably in bed early in the morning on the day that, in her dream, she had thrown the bag of poop over at the new house.

The house. It all came back to the house.

Now that she knew she was dreaming she felt *so* relieved and pushed up on her tiptoes and tried to start flying.

No liftoff.

She checked to see if she was wearing pants (yes) or her teeth were loose (no).

Ah, well. In just a bit Arnold would wake her up and … Arnold, who didn't have to go to the vet. That was good. She used her hands to tap her cheeks.

"Wake up! Okay. Wake up now!"

No, not yet. Apparently. In the meantime and just for fun, she'd come up with a few of the questions she had for Miriam.

Was that the name of a character in a movie she'd recently watched?

Okay. She pulled out her cellphone and tapped the record app. "Questions for Miriam. One: If you're the Virgin Mary why aren't you wearing blue. Isn't that your thing?"

Good. She resumed walking at a pleasant pace and worked on her list. A distracting way to pass the time until—really at home and in her bed—Arnold would lick her face or bump her leg.

2. Why did you come to *me*?

3. I've seen you eat and drink but do you ever need to use the bathroom?

4. Are you everywhere on earth right now and in my kitchen? And in heaven?

5. Why snickerdoodles?

6. How old were you when you got preg …

Debra stopped partway through number six when she saw Yvonne Billings crying, gasping, sniffing, and smoking. Her friend was leaning against a car outside the family's home.

Clearly distraught. She wiped her eyes with the fingers of her non-cigarette hand and waved.

"What's going on?" Debra asked, walking toward her.

"I don't know. Where's Arnold? I don't know. I had to get out. I had to … . I guess I'm a bad daughter. My sister is on her way. I um I um … "

"Here," Debra said taking her arm. "We'll sit here on the porch steps." She guided the woman down, sat next to her, linked her arm in hers, and said. "Your mom?"

Yvonne nodded, flipped her cigarette butt into the yard, turned, and collapsed onto Debra's chest. Into Debra's arms.

"I should be with her. What kind of daughter am I! But I just had to get some air. I just had to have a goddamn cigarette. I'm the worst … "

"Your mom," Debra said. "Has she … ?"

Yvonne wailed into the front of Debra's coat. She rocked forward and back, and Debra moved with her.

Her mom.

Mrs. McConkey.

16

Debra stayed until Yvonne's sister showed up. About twenty minutes. Raced up. Parked at a crazy angle. Left the car door open. Said, "Oh, Vonnie." And took Debra's place.

Leaning on each other for support, they stood up and headed inside and Debra headed home.

Question number 7. "What the fu ... ?"

Arnold barking and jumping. The air filled with the aroma of freshly baked cookies. Miriam sitting in the living room.

"What in theee hell!" Debra demanded.

"It's okay," Miriam said softly.

"Bullhonkey it's okay. I ask you to ask Jesus to help an old lady and he kills her? Thanks for nothing."

It was a minute, a solid sixty seconds, of Debra ranting, venting, cursing, questioning. ("Anti-religioning"?)

Miriam said nothing, absorbed everything. Took it. Just took it. Her face showing nothing but compassion.

Then a tear. One tear. From her right eye and down her right cheek.

"Death is so hard," she whispered. "So very, very hard."

Debra stared down at her. No mini-sermon. No talk of

God's will, God's way. Of faith.

Here was a woman familiar with death.

"Big Jay and Little Jay," Debra said. Realized.

"Very, very hard," Miriam said.

"But you … you're Miriam. Mary. You … ."

"My husband died. My son was arrested, tortured, and executed."

"Jesus!" An interjection. "Sorry, but Jesus!" Another interjection. "How can you be so … freaking … sweet. Kind. Loving. Forgiving."

Debra paused.

"So helpful," she continued. "You've got it made. Why in hell, in the name of heaven, would you be *helpful?* It. Makes. No. Sense."

"Where do you want me to start?" She wiped her cheek and then wiped her fingers on the leg of her pants.

Debra sat down. "Sorry I kind of blew up."

"'Kind of,'" Miriam said and smiled.

"Yeah," Debra said. "You should see me when I'm really honked off." Taking the lighthearted cue from her guest.

"I have."

"Uh … buh … "

"Relax. It's okay. Like Little Jay said to me one time as he pointed at Big Jay. 'Well, we can't all be perfect.'"

"He did not!" Debra said.

"Would I tell a lie?"

Silence.

"Check and mate," Miriam said. Then: "So tell me about Margaret's daughters."

"Who?"

"Mrs. McConkey."

"They're blown away."

Miriam nodded.

"I don't know what that's like," Debra said. "When my parents … passed away … I was deep into … a time of my life that I'm really not proud of."

Miriam gave another little nod.

"Their deaths are just a part of, a piece of … ." She shrugged. "I couldn't have been there. with them. I mean, no matter what. A car accident. Both just … gone. I guess Dad died first. Then just a little bit later, Mom. So she died alone."

Miriam shook her head.

"Now and at the hour of our death. Amen," she said, reciting the last phrase of the Hail Mary prayer.

Debra gasped. Again and again.

"You were there," she said and Miriam reached forward and took her hand.

"I was."

"Dear God, dear God, dear God."

Miriam squeezed Debra's hand.

"Her final prayer, her final request, on earth, was that I help you. I'm here to help you."

17

It was too much. Just too much.

Debra had stood up, walked stiffly into her room, shut the door, and flopped on the bed. Through the morning, afternoon, evening, nighttime. Getting up to use the bathroom To get a drink of water. Not awake but not sleeping.

Too much. It was just too much.

For the first time in a long time three fingers of scotch sounded so appealing.

Finally, she slept.

Not moving. Not dreaming.

She woke to the sound of Arnold doing his *arrr-ruuu-ruuu* bark that had the cadence of someone talking.

"We're going to wait for Debra" she heard Miriam say.

"*Arrr.*" This with an up-and-down tone and rhythm.

"I know, but I'm not having any either. We can wait."

"*Arr.*"

"That's a good boy."

The dog sneezed.

"God bless you."

Debra slowly shuffled out to the kitchen and, it seemed, Arnold couldn't be happier to see her.

"Coffee?" Miriam said.

A little nod.

"Toast? Jam? Marmalade? Eggs?"

"Sure. Toast. Jam. Scrambled."

"*Arrrrrrrr!*" This from Arnold. Apparently meaning "Yes, please."

Miriam got to work, Debra plopped down on a kitchen chair, Arnold thumped his head in her lap.

"I'm so sorry," Miriam said, keeping her eyes on the frying pan.

Debra shrugged.

"I could have handled that better," Miriam said. "That was a lot to take in."

Debra sighed. Arnold looked up at her face.

"No. There was no easy way to say all that. No easy way to hear it."

"I just wanted you to know ... "

"I know. Mom wasn't alone. Dad wasn't alone and then Mom wasn't alone. Thank you. For doing that. And for telling me. It just has to kind of sink in."

"You don't realize it but you're very kind, too," Miriam said and Debra grunted. Arnold gave her a closer look.

"I don't think so," Debra said. "That's ... " *What was the expression?* " ... not in my wheelhouse."

Time passed. As it always does.

Miriam set a plate of food in front of Debra and scooped some scrambled eggs into Arnold's food bowl.

He inhaled them.

Debra fed him half a slice of toast.

Two chews and down.

"Kind to others," Miriam said. "And to Arnold. Pretty tough on yourself."

"Yeah. Well."

"Not a criticism," Miriam said. "Just an observation."

"Uh huh."

"Would you like me to leave?"

Debra shrugged.

"It's okay," Miriam said. "Really. I never want to force myself on anyone."

Silence. For a time. Then:

"No," Debra said. "Not until the marmalade's gone. I bought it because it was on sale. Had forgotten I don't like it."

"Oh. Well. Please let me do you the favor of finishing off your marmalade."

"Sure."

Neither woman spoke but Arnold asked for more toast. They ignored him and he gave up.

Then, not lifting her eyes, Debra said: "My mom. How was she … ?"

"She wasn't afraid," Miriam said. "Not for your dad or for herself."

Debra nodded. "She was a brave woman."

"The last thing she said to me, on earth, was "'Please take care of my girls.'"

The only sounds in the room the refrigerator motor, Arnold's stomach, and Debra' single, soft sob.

18

Neither woman spoke for a time and then Debra shudder-sighed deeply, picked up a paper napkin off the table and used it to wipe her eyes and blow her nose.

Miriam got up, topped off Debra's coffee cup, and gave a quarter piece of toast to Arnold. "Last one," she told him. "Chew slowly and enjoy."

He ignored her suggestion.

"I still don't know if you're real," Miriam said. "I'm so tired."

Again, a quiet room.

"I'm going back to bed. Thank you for breakfast."

She had a little trouble getting to her feet.

"Arnold, nap time."

The dog didn't need to be told twice.

She lay on her back with Arnold next to her. His head resting on her stomach. Her hand gently rubbing his fur.

She heard Miriam go downstairs.

It was all … so much.

Too much.

"It makes no sense," she whispered, not disturbing

Arnold. "It's senseless. I've lost my senses. I've had, what is it called?, some kind of mental breakdown.

"Something snapped when you and I were out on the porch and I threw the bag and then reality left. Up, up, and away."

Arnold burped as he slept.

Eggs. She could smell eggs.

But she hadn't cooked any eggs this morning. Had she? She hadn't fixed breakfast. Had she?

How did a person know if they were thinking clearly when they weren't sure they were thinking clearly?

Mom and Dad.

The crash.

Getting the news. The horrid, horrid, terrifying news.

Funeral home. Mass of Christian burial. Two gaping holes. Side by side. Graveside service.

Her husband and oh-so young daughter there, but the three of them no longer a family.

Oblivion. Bits and pieces and blurs. Numbness and pain, simultaneously.

Still a wife and mother. Her child. A little girl who … .

Comfort. No, not comfort. Dullness. Dull. No sharp edge. Taking the edge off. Harder to get there. Taking more effort. More …

Booze. Drugs. Men. Nameless, faceless, pawing … .

Dancing into hell.

Rolling away from … .

Mom had been so brave.

Dad had been so good.

She was such a …

What had stirred this up? Why now?

Well, either her mind had snapped or the mother of God was in her basement.

Which seemed more likely?

She didn't remember drifting into sleep but then she woke up.

A decision.

Why not?

Why not be her mother's daughter?

Why not be brave? Stupid, perhaps. Mentally ill, most likely. But brave.

19

"Would you like to go for a walk?" Debra asked and Arnold raced to the front door.

"I meant you," she said to Miriam, both women sitting in the living room. "Not just him."

"Thank you. That would be great."

"There's this little place about a mile and a half from here. For lunch. My treat."

"You are so sweet! I'll get my coat."

"Wally's," Debra said to Arnold. He jumped in agreement with the plan. Its dog-loving owner welcomed furry four-legged patrons.

"I've made a decision," Debra said when the three of them were about three-quarters of a mile from home. Miriam holding Arnold's leash.

"Oh?"

"Either I'm losing my mind, or you're really here and you're really who you say you are."

"Uh huh."

"So I'm just going with plan B."

"Oh, good."

"Okay, well, I have some questions. Some more questions."

"Fire away."

"Do you ever have to go to the bathroom?"

Miriam stopped midstride, Arnold abruptly did the same on the far end of his leash, and Debra said, "I'm sorry. I don't know what got … "

"No, no. It's just that after almost two thousand years of popping in all around the globe, you're the first one who asked me that."

"I really am … "

"You should get a medal. Really. I'll have to work on that."

They resumed walking.

"So," Miriam said, "the answer is no. I eat and drink but don't … And, no, I don't know why."

"Okay. Enough of that. Are you only here or are you someplace else right now, too?"

"A lot of places. A lot of people."

"And they're getting a visit like I am?"

"No-o-o-o, this isn't typical."

"So what is?"

"Oh, I give them comfort, speak to them in their hearts. Maybe a—I suppose you could call it minor—vision. See me but there's no interaction like with you and me."

"So why me?"

"You'll see."

"Well, that's vague enough to be true."

"No. Really. I promise."

A quarter mile more of walking.

"So," Debra said, "do you always look the same or sound the same when you visit someone?"

"I dress for the occasion."

"So I'm … informal," Debra said.

"And your initial greeting really would have messed things up if I had been wearing a golden crown. Probably would have split the bag wide open."

"I … !"

"I told you the archangels laughed, right?"

Debra didn't say anything.

"Enough teasing," Miriam said. "I think the best way to explain it is I look and sound like a person's mom or grandma. An aunt, female teacher or coach, older sister. Someone like that was, or still is, a part of their life. A woman they know and trust and love. There's a familiarity there. A family bond in the widest definition of family."

"But … "

"I promise: you'll see."

Then: "Debra! Debra!"

20

The trio looked ahead toward the shouting.

"Yvonne Billings," Debra said. "Mrs. McConkey's daughter. You prayed for the mom."

Not adding: "But that didn't work."

They were two houses from the McConkey house. Where Debra had been ... when?

Yvonne hurried down the front porch steps and gave Debra a fierce hug. Arnold hopped up on his hind legs and joined in.

"It's all just a blur," Yvonne said. "I'm so sad. I'm so relieved. Does that sound awful? I'm awful."

She pulled back, still holding Debra but now face-to-face.

"Thank God my sister is here, too. The organizer. Take charge. Since we were kids. I'm in kind of a dream state and then at some points a nightmare state. And I'm drinking a lot of coffee and smoking a lot. Kinda wired."

She gave a deep sigh. Debra getting smacked in the face with the odors of both. Then the woman noticed Miriam.

"Oh," Yvonne said. "I didn't see ... "

"For you," Miriam said holding up a pink bakery box with a variety of pastries showing through its cellophane window.

"Well, aren't you sweet! I'm Yvonne. Vonnie. And you must think I'm crazy."

"It's hard to lose a mom," Miriam aid, "no matter how old she is or you are." Then barely getting the cardboard box handed off to Debra as Yvonne let go of one woman and began seriously hugging the other.

Arnold doing his best to get his nose right up against the box.

"You are *so* right!" Yvonne said. "Losing Mom is ... ." Her voice trailed off.

"It sucks," Debra said, doing her best to keep Arnold away from the pastries.

"It does! It just does. Even though Mom had a long, full life and had been asking God to take her for at least the last two years. Sick and tired of being sick and tired. Wanted to be with Dad."

Then the tears came. The sobs. Miriam laid the woman's head on her shoulder, patting and rubbing her back.

"Death is so hard," Miriam said softly. "It's just so hard."

Arnold stopped jumping at the box.

Sat down.

Watched quietly.

"*Rurrr.*"

Yvonne's sister—Debra couldn't remember her name—called from the front door.

"Coming!" Yvonne answered. Sniffed with gusto. Shook her head. Wiped her eyes. "Whoo. Bleah." Smiled. "Thanks for the treats. And the hugs."

A deep sigh then quickly back into the house.

"Come on, Arnold," Miriam said, giving the leash a little tug. "Wally's."

The dog refocused hearing the name of the diner and began leading Miriam toward it. Debra followed.

"I have more questions," Debra said.

"I bet you do.

21

The diner had everything a diner should have and nothing it shouldn't. Seated about thirty people. It's owner, Juan, had kept the place's name because—as he often told customers: "Why should I pay good money for a new sign?"

No one argued with his logic.

Arnold had been first through the door and headed straight to "his" spot under "their" table.

A busy waitress, of Debra's vintage, nodded her greeting and then took a second look at Miriam. Someone new. Or maybe not.

"I love little places like this," Miriam said after they had sat down facing each other in the booth.

"Eat out much?"

"You'd be surprised."

"Oh, I don't know that you can surprise me anymore."

"Wanna bet?" Miriam teased.

A look crossed Debra's face."

"No, no, no," Miriam said. "It'll be okay."

"'Will be'?"

"Big Jay used to say, 'There are enough worries for today. Don't go chasing tomorrow's.'"

"Only he said it in Hebrew," Debra said.

"Aramaic."

The waitress came up and bent over to look under the table. "Morning, you big dumb dog."

Arnold grunted.

She straightened up and smiled. Then to Miriam: "Have you been in here before?"

"No. It's great."

"Have we met?"

"Oh, I suspect our paths have crossed," she said. "And I just have one of those faces."

The waitress—"Beth" on her uniform shirt— nodded. "I s'pose."

"How you doing, Debra?"

"Oh, you know." She shrugged.

"Is your full name Elizabeth?" Miriam asked the waitress.

"Yeah."

"That a pretty name. It means 'God is my abundance.'"

"Yeah?"

"I had a cousin named Elizabeth. Well, family member. Lot of 'cousins.'" She made air quotations marks.

Debra rolled her eyes.

The waitress patted Miriam's hand. "Me, too." She nodded toward the kitchen. "And Juan? Jesus Christ, he has more … "

Debra cleared her throat.

"Oh, right. Ready to order?" Then, leaning in a little toward Miriam: "And some of them named Jesus. Hay-zoos."

"Another good name," Miriam said. "Any Josés?"

"Si, si, si."

"Marias?"

"You bet."

"Lovely"

"So, Debra" said, "I'll have … "

The food arrived. Bacon, eggs, and toast for Debra.

Miriam with a Belgian waffle, extra whipped cream. Arnold having some, but not enough, from both plates. Plus some dog biscuits from Beth.

The women agreed breakfast wasn't limited to breakfast.

"Any Pontius Pilates?" Debra said, imitating Miriam's voice, as they began eating.

"I love meeting people."

"But you know everyone."

"Confusing, isn't it?" Miriam said.

"Apparently not for you."

A look crossed Debra's face. A light bulb going off.

"So Yvonne and Beth can see you?"

"See me? Of course."

"So this isn't a—what?—exclusive visit?"

"Oh, but you're my favorite," Miriam said, lightly teasing.

"Uh huh. So if I'm going crazy they are, too."

"That makes sense."

Debra had more of her eggs. Slipped Arnold a bit of toast with raspberry jam on it.

Which was instantly gone.

"Is it always like this?" Debra asked.

"It varies."

"Why?"

"People vary. Circumstances vary."

"What if I tell Beth you're the mother of God?"

Miriam shrugged.

"I could you know."

"You could."

"You think I won't? Debra asked.

"Up to you. Free will."

"Okay, I will.

"Okay."

22

"Miriam is Mary, the mother of God," Debra said to Beth as the waitress dropped the check on their table.

"Okay. Thanks for coming in." And off to fill other patrons' coffee cups.

"I've got this," Miriam said, picking up the slip of paper. "You take care of the tip."

"Okay," Debra said, imitating Beth. Then, as Miriam started to get up: "Wait! What if I stand on a chair and announce to everyone in here that you're Mary, the mother of God."

"Free will."

"But?"

"But they'd think it's a bad joke, you're tipsy, or you're not of sound mind."

"I'll tell them about the pink box. The pastries. Out of nowhere."

Miriam looked at her. Patience. Compassion.

Arnold tried to stand up under the table, bonked his head, gave a little yelp, crawled out, and stood up.

"You'd tell them it was the truth," Debra said. "You wouldn't lie."

"I wouldn't lie."

"But?"

"Then they'd think you're a fool and I'm some kind of a con artist trying to take advantage of you. Oh, I'm as off-kilter as you are. Debra and the crazy Black lady."

Debra thought about that. Arnold started getting antsy.

"Sounds like a TV show," she said.

"Comedy."

"Oh, yeah."

"How come I get second billing?"

"Thought you'd be used to it," Debra said.

"Oh?" Playing along.

"'Jesus and Mary.'"

Once again, Debra noticed her lovely smile

"Nice," Miriam said. "Very good."

"Do I get another medal?" Debra asked.

"Let's not be greedy," Miriam said. "It's unseemly. Two, but only once for you."

They walked home in the shared, comfortable silence of two longtime friends. Words not somehow forbidden but, here and now, not needed. Enjoying—savoring—each other's company. Each other's presence.

And Arnold a part of it.

It was the knocking at the front door that woke up Debra in the middle of that night. Small but urgent. Five taps and then some words. Unclear. A young voice. A child's?

Arnold looked over at Debra. "I don't know," she said. Unconsciously whispering because it was dark.

Tap, tap, tap, tap, tap. Words.

She got up and, without turning on a light, walked to the front door in here sweatshirt and pajama pants. She looked out the door's fisheye peephole.

Nothing.

Flicked on the porch light and looked again.

No one.

Tap, tap, tap, tap, tap. "Mommy won't wake up."

Debra heard a noise behind her and jumped.

"Sorry," Miriam whispered.

Tap, tap, tap, tap, tap. "Mommy won't wake up." This a little louder. The fear in her voice now clear.

"Worthless guard dog," Debra said at Arnold who was standing behind Miriam.

Tap, tap … Debra opened the door.

A little girl. Black. Maybe four years old. Wide-eyed. Terrified. "MOMMY WON'T WAKE UP!"

"Where's Mommy?" Miriam said, now next to Debra and down on one knee.

The girl turned and pointed at a car stopped at a crazy angle two houses down. One front fender almost touching the neighbor's wooden fence. Lights off. Engine off.

23

Debra scooped the child up in her arms and hurried down the steps, across the yard, and toward the car.

"What's your name, honey?"

"Shelley,"

"Okay, Shelley. Your mommy's going to be okay."

As they got closer, Debra spotted a woman behind the steering wheel slumped over toward the open passenger door.

Shelley saw her, too.

"Mommy!"

"Here," Miriam said. Behind them, arms open. Debra passed the little girl to her and leaned into the car.

Eyes closed. No movement. No sound. Then a short breath immediately followed by deep, deep hacking cough. A kind Debra had never heard before. One that went on and on.

"You saying prayers?" Debra shouted into the woman's face but directed toward Miriam.

"Yes."

"You have a cellphone?"

"No."

"Well, sh ... "

The woman opened eyes that didn't focus.

Booze? No. No smell.

Drugs? Maybe. Some new synthetic kind developed after Debra's time.

"Let's get her inside," Miriam said.

"Let's call nine one one."

"Inside first. I'm sure."

A moment. Two moments.

"Fine," Debra said. She reached across the woman and unlocked the driver door.

Looking back, at three in the morning, Debra had no idea how the two sixty-plus-year-olds got the woman out of the car, up the porch steps, and into Debra's bed.

She had no memory of where Arnold had been during all this.

Or why she hadn't called an aid car.

After a time, seeing that her mother was someplace safe and sound asleep, the child nodded off on the sofa with Miriam sitting in an armchair pulled up next to it. Arnold dozed at her feet.

Debra sat in the other chair. Her eyes closed but unable to sleep at all. Well, maybe some. Bits and pieces that felt like none.

"Your mom is a ... take-charge kind of gal." This not directed at Shelley but at Miriam's son. Little Jay. Hay-zoos.

Huh.

"My first prayer since I don't know when but I suppose you do." This also to Jesus. "So. What's new?"

No reply.

"Whole lotta shakin' going on down here. I am so tired."

"From the heart," Miriam said to Debra. Startling her. "Just beautiful." She wiped her eyes, found a tissue in her pants pocket and quietly blew her nose.

"This reeks of 'God's plan,'" Debra said.

"His ways are mysterious." This with a double raising of

her eyebrows.

"Or maybe they're just cockamamie but he pulls it off in the end."

"Maybe."

"How old is she?" A nod toward the girl.

"Four. Five in July."

"Four-and-a-half. The 'half' is a big deal when you're four."

"A big deal," Miriam agreed.

"Course it's been a while since I was that age and you, you! More than two thousand years ago."

"True."

"I assume you use anti-aging cream. Care to share?"

"You're tired."

"I am."

"A little winey."

Debra squinted at her. "Whiny?" It was true, at best, but still . . .

"No. Like wine. Like a little rummy."

"Oh. Yeah."

"Go on upstairs and get a bit of sleep in the guest room."

"You see the irony in that statement, right?"

"And like it."

She pushed the junk off the guestroom bed and lay down. Felt like she could have slept forever.

Got forty-five minutes before the noise woke her. The voices.

24

Debra barely opened her eyes. Still dark out. But the window was in the wrong place. And the noise. Not construction on the house. She closed her eyes, rolled over ...

"You flooded it."

"Said Noah to the Lord," a second voice said.

"I didn't." A third voice. "It won't start."

1: "You mean you can't start it."

2: "Remember when he couldn't get that donkey to move?"

1:"That was hil*ar*ious!"

2: Still is."

3:"Can we just get this done?"

1: "Why not just a little ... zazoo-zazz ... and it's right where it's supposed to be?"

3: "I don't know."

2: "Then what good are you?"

3: "That comment gets old."

1. "It's timeless."

3: "But today isn't. We need to get this car moved before the sun comes up."

2: "The sun *is* up."

3: (with a bit of edge to his voice) "When the sun is up on *this* street."

Debra opened her eyes all the way. A car? The street?

She sat up on the side of the bed and then gave a tired grunt as she stood. To the window. Peeked out the blinds.

Three men. Early twenties. Big. Work clothes. Faces indiscernible in the dark. One guy in the car, behind the wheel. The others standing by the front fender almost touching the fence.

"Just push me." Voice three. Guy in the car.

"You mean push the car?" Voice two.

"All right, all right. You ready?" Voice one.

Guys 1 and 2 leaned on the front of the hood and pushed. Nothing.

3: "Come on! Push!"

1:"Uh, Mikey?"

2: "You want to take your foot off the brake pedal?"

3: "My foot isn't … "

1: "That red glow behind the car? It's from the brake lights."

Laughter from 1 and 2.

1: "You got the clutch in?"

3: "It's an automatic."

1: "Got it in neutral?"

3: "Y… Wait. Okay. Yeah."

1: (speaking to 2) "You think anyone else is seeing all this?"

2: "Oh, I hope so."

3: "Can we just get this done? Push the car back all the way into the street, then go behind it and push it so it's in front the lady's house. Parallel to her fence."

2: "'Parallel'? That's some mighty fancy talkin' there, that's what that is."

1: (giving 2's arm a little shove) "Look, the sooner we … Wait!" Pulling 2 some ten feet away from the car. Then to 3, the guy behind the wheel: "Put 'er in park, you got the keys, right?" Apparently a nod from the guy inside. Then: "Crank it!"

Some mechanical sounds and then an engine coming to life.

1 and 2: (looking at each other) "Flooded."

The driver backing it up and turning to straighten it so he could easily park—parallel–in front of Debra's fence. The other two guys sauntering down the street toward it.

2: (pointing at the car) "Well, looky, looky. I hadn't noticed."

1: "What?"

3 now out of the car—bigger than the other two—practically flying past the house under construction, and starting to round the corner.

2: "The make of the car. Son, I think that there is a 2020 Donkey."

And at this point in Debra's week, the scene seemed pretty much normal.

She slid back into bed and fell asleep.

25

Debra woke a little after eight. Still groggy but okay. A trip to the bathroom and then downstairs. Miriam and Shelley at the kitchen table.

So that part—a kid and a mom—wasn't a dream. What was? She thought about it for a moment. The guys and the car. Weird.

"Mommy is sleeping," Shelley said. "We peeked in."

Miriam nodded. "She needs her rest."

"Yes," Shelley said, sounding very adult. "She needs her rest."

"*Rurr,*" From Arnold, lying at the girl's feet.

"Good," Debra said. "Sometimes rest is the best medicine."

"That's what Mommy says."

"That's what my mom used to say."

Shelley seemed to be thinking about that.

"Waffle?" This from Miriam.

"Again?"

"When in Rome."

"They're good," Shelley said. "Arnold likes them, too."

"Oh, he does," Debra said.

She gave Miriam a look that she hoped the mother of God could rightly interpret as "so what's the plan here?" Then thinking: *Our plan. Not God's plan or God will. But just what the ... What are we supposed to do with a little kid and her mom, who is sick and sleeping in my bed?*

"Did you hear them?" Shelley asked?

"Them?" Debra said.

"The ones moving Mommy's car. They woke me."

"Me, too."

So it had been real.

Of course.

Why not?

"They were funny," Shelley said.

Huh. Debra hadn't thought about that part of it. "Yeah, they were."

"One of them called Mommy's car a donkey."

Debra smiled. "He did."

"They're friends of Mim." This with a nod toward Miriam. Obviously a term of endearment.

"Oh?" Debra said with another look at Miriam.

"Old friends," Shelley said. "I'm a new friend."

"Uh huh."

"Of her and ... I don't remember your name."

"Debra."

"You're helping Mommy."

Well, crud.

"I'm glad I can," she lied. Thought about that and then grudgingly corrected herself. A half-truth? A quarter-truth?

"Mim says people have been eating waffles for a million years."

"She would know."

"Hundreds of years," Miriam said gently.

"For hundreds of years."

"Uh huh," Debra said, pouring herself a cup coffee.

"You know why these are the best?"

"Huh uh." *Come on caffeine, do your thing.*

"Cuz they're always the best when you eat them with a friend."

"Or whip cream," Debra said and Miriam gave a laugh-snort.

Shelley looked alarmed and then smiled a wide smile and imitated her.

Arnold stood and look around. No bacon. Back to resting on the floor.

"Oh, my goodness, pardon me," Miriam said.

Shelley gave another laugh-snort and a surprisingly good imitation of Miriam, saying, "Oh, my goodness, pardon me."

Debra couldn't help smiling.

A nice kid.

When was she leaving. Were *they* leaving? Shelley and the woman in the bedroom.

"Do you want a waffle?" Shelley asked. A little hostess.

"Maybe later."

"We made you one. You just have to heat it up."

"Okay."

"Now?" Shelley asked Miriam.

She nodded. "Now. With Debra." Then to Debra: "The three of us are going to take another little peek at Mommy."

26

Debra really didn't want to, but then the kid popped up, took her hand, and started to lead her toward the bedroom.

God da ... bless it.

Miriam walked behind them.

"This is how you peek," Shelley said softly. Taking small, careful steps on her tiptoes.

"Sneak," Debra said without thinking about it. "First we sneak and then we peek."

"Sneak and peek," Shelley said.

"You like that?"

"Sneak and peek, sneak and peek, sneak and peek." She slowly turned the doorknob, opened the door a few inches, and gasped.

"Mommy!" She rushed in, dragging Debra with her.

The woman tried to lift her arms but only managed to raise them slightly.

She's really been put through the ringer, Debra thought. *Now there's an old expression. She's still going through the ringer.*

Shelley dropped Debra's hand, raced to her mother, and snuggled between her arms, getting a near-lifeless but fully-loving hug.

"I was scared," Shelley said.

"You were brave," her mom softly answered. "You did a good job."

"Mommy."

"Shelley."

"Are you all better now?"

"I'm getting better, honey."

The little girl began rocking herself, and to a small degree her mother, back and forth, almost chanting:

"Shelley, Mommy. Shelley, Mommy. Shelley, Mommy."

Her mother's eyes closed. "I just need a little nap," She barely whispered and was asleep.

"It's okay," Debra said, coming forward and putting her hands on Shelley's shoulders. "Mommy needs a little more rest."

"The best medicine," Shelley said, giving two more back-and-forth rocks and then standing fully up and taking a step away from the bed.

Debra turned her toward the door and they walked out together. Shelley pulled the door almost-closed. Leaving it cracked just enough that she could easily peek in.

"Will you help me?" Miriam asked her.

She nodded. "I'm brave."

"You are."

"I got Mommy help."

"You did."

"I did a good job."

"An excellent job."

"Excellent," Shelley agreed and looked at Debra, who nodded.

"Did your mommy cook this, too?" Shelley asked Miriam.

Fifteen minutes later. Back in the kitchen. A variety of ingredients spread all over the counters and table. The majority of them, Debra was certain, had not been in her cupboards or refrigerator.

"Not a lot of chicken dishes," Miriam said. "More fish."

"And chips?"

"No, no chips. Bread."

The girl thought about that.

"Tartar sauce?"

Miriam shook her head.

More thought.

"Did people like that?"

Miriam nodded. "At one … picnic … I saw whole bunches of them eat it."

"How many?"

"Oh … thousands and thousands."

Shelly laughed. Such silliness.

"Tell her about the wine," Debra said. Leaning against a counter and eating her second warmed-up waffle.

Miriam smiled. "That was quite a party," she said.

"So that stuff is true?"

"Helps if you were there. Easier to believe it."

"Uh huh."

Shelley interrupted them: "I never made … What do you call this?"

"Authentic Jewish chicken soup. Another item on the 'best medicine' list."

"Are you … What was that word?"

"Jewish. Yes, I'm Jewish, just like my mommy and daddy."

"My mommy is American," Shelley said. "Daddy is 'Hay-sun.'"

"Haitian."

"Yeah. Hay-shun. *Mon père.*"

Debra looked surprised by the French.

"He got ported," Shelley said.

"Deported," Miriam said.

"Yeah. Deeee-ported."

Debra looked at Miriam who gave her a slight nod. A slight "I'll explain this to you later" nod.

27

Again, as always, time passed. A few hours. The kitchen smelled like soup. Debra assumed the whole house did. All three of them Miriam, Shelley, and Debra—had put together an authentic Jewish mother's chicken noodle soup.

It smelled *good.*

It looked *good.*

It tasted *outstanding.*

They were back at the kitchen table. Sampling.

Arnold had already rated it Five Slurps.

Debra hadn't bothered asking where the ingredients had come from. Miriam would have said "They were in the back of the cupboard" or "They were in the back of the refrigerator."

Which, Debra was sure, was the truth. Miriam didn't lie. But it wasn't the *whole* truth, which she assumed was:

"I put them in the cupboard/refrigerator and they were in the back of the cupboard/refrigerator."

There for how long? Ten seconds?

Debra was certain she never had a big, fat whole chicken in her refrigerator. Or a box of matzo meal in her cupboard. She had never heard of matzo meal.

A key ingredient in matzo balls.

Which were a key ingredient in chicken matzo ball soup.

The whole, long process had kept Shelley busy ... and chattering about everything and nothing.

"This isn't a recipe from old Palestine days, is it?" Debra asked Miriam.

"One picks up things along the way," Miriam said, "and retains the good ones. It is the soup of my people."

"You're Jewish," Debra said, still surprised by that and surprised that it surprised her.

"Right. Born and bred."

"I think my mother would claim you're Irish."

"Oh, that too. You know. 'Mom' to everyone so ... " She shrugged and then leaned toward Debra and whispered:

"I wasn't a cradle Catholic." She paused and made a startled oh-no! face. "I'm a convert." A gasp. Repeated the face.

Debra couldn't help laughing. Shelley, not understanding any of it, joined it.

Miriam held her right index finger straight up and shook it a little bit. "There's more! So were all the boys."

"What boys?" Shelley asked. Finally a word she was sure of.

"The twelve boys. Dear friends of my boy."

"You have a boy!" Shelley said. "How old is he?"

"Oh ... he's all grown up."

Shelley's interest level dropped but there was enough left to ask: "What's his name?"

"Little Jay."

"Who's Big Jay?"

"My husband."

"Oh." No interest. Then: "Can we give Mommy some soup?"

"Probably just broth for now."

Shelley's face registered "Huh?"

"The liquid, the watery part," Debra said.

"There's a little bit cooling in a mug on the counter," Miriam said. She stood, opened the magical/mystical refrigerator's door, and pulled out a small bottle of an electrolytes-packed sports drink.

"And this is for her, too."

"What is it?"

"It helps you when you're sick."

"Like Jewish soup?"

"Yes."

"It's Jewish pop?"

Both women managed not to laugh. Miriam turned her head and her shoulders shook. Debra stepped into the living room and heard, from the bedroom:

"Shelley? Honey? Shelley?"

Shelley's young ears heard it, too. She blew past Debra and into the bedroom. No sneaking, no peeking.

Debra quickly followed. Then Arnold. Then Miriam, with a mug of broth in her right hand and a bottle of the sports drink in her left.

"Mommy," Shelley said, back in her mother's arms that seemed to have a little more strength in them. The mother halfway sitting up.

"Shelley."

"Mommy."

"Shelley."

"Mommy."

"Mommy" the mother said and Shelley pulled back to look at her. She was looking at Debra.

"Mommy," the woman said and Debra stared ... then staggered.

28

It's amazing how quickly guilt can flood a mind.

Catholic guilt. Jewish guilt. Any race, color, creed, nationality, ethnicity, sexual orientation … guilt.

Son or daughter guilt. Sibling guilt. Extended-family guilt. Parent guilt.

Mother guilt.

Mother guilt, the Mother of All Guilts.

She hadn't recognized her own daughter.

Her own *daughter.*

What kind of a …

No, she knew what kind of a …

She was even worse than—for so many years—what she thought she was.

She was *the* worst.

Ever.

Ever, ever, ever.

She began to cry.

To sob.

To beyond sob.

"The worst. The worst. The worst," she managed between gasps.

"Shelley," the woman said. "That's your grandma."

The little girl turned and, obviously, was looking at Miriam.

Miriam shook her head, set the mug on a dresser, stepped forward, stood side-by-side with Debra, and put her right arm around Debra's shoulders.

A moment passed. Three moments. Five.

Then Miriam handed Debra the bottle of sports drink and slid a straw into it. She led, walked with, Debra to the side of the bed opposite Shelley and waited.

The sobbing had stopped. The tears hadn't. Now they were in the woman's eyes, too.

In the eyes of Debra's daughter.

In Emily's eyes.

Emmy's.

Debra bent over, helped her sit up a little more, and eased the straw into Emily's mouth. The younger woman drank, her eyes never leaving her mother's face. Her mother's eyes.

Like when she was an infant. Eyes on me. Same eyes.

If this was another dream, Debra wanted to wake up and never wake up. If all of this, all of the way back to the poop bag hitting Miriam's head ... .

"Is it good?" Shelley asked her mom.

"Very good." Quietly.

"We made soup for you," the four-year-old said. "Jewish soup. With chicken and lotsa balls."

All the women in the room smiled little smiles.

"Me and Mim and ... I forget her name."

As well you should.

"Debra," Miriam said.

Shelley thought about that.

"Mommy's mommy."

"Yes," Miriam said.

"My ... ?"

"Grandma."

More thought. Eyes squinting in concentration. Then:

"We made soup for you. Me and Mim and Gramma Debby."

Again Debra staggered. This time spilling sports drink on the bed.

A pause.

"Are you up to having a little broth?" Miriam asked Emily.

"Yes. Thank you."

Miriam took the bottle from Debra, pulled a paper napkin from her pocket, wiped the bed, stepped to the dresser, and exchanged the bottle for the mug.

Again, she stood next to Debra. Handed her the mug. Without thinking Debra dipped her finger into the broth. Warm. Not hot.

Good.

She bent over and held the mug next to Emily's lips. The younger woman tried to raise her hands to help hold it but lacked the strength.

Debra slightly tipped the rim and her daughter drank.

One sip.

A second.

A third.

A fourth.

Debra fed her daughter.

"More?" Debra asked.

Emily shook her head. "It's very, very good," she told her daughter. "You're a good cook."

"We'll teach you how to make it," Shelley said and Emily nodded.

Smiled.

Nodded off.

29

It was the faintest tinge of normalcy. Fifteen minutes later. Debra taking Arnold for an afternoon walk. Or Arnold taking Debra for one.

Just the two of them. Arnold—sniffing items and places with wild abandon—at peace. Debra ...

"It's like a giant ball of ... what?" she said. Arnold looking back at her when he heard the word "ball."

No ball. No matter.

"A giant ball of I don't know what."

This time Arnold not taking the bate.

Debra: So happy to see Emmy. So happy to meet Shelley.

"You could have knocked me over with a feather. One of Mom's expressions.

"It did knock me. For a loop.

"Mom used to say that, too."

Mom: A great-grandmother. God rest her soul.

Shelley ...

"So sharp," Debra told Arnold. "Sharp as a tack."

They walked past three more houses.

"And sweet. Sweet as pie."

No reaction from Arnold. Not familiar with that pastry.

Past two more house. Five. Ten.

"I gave my baby girl something to drink this morning," Debra said.

"I fed her ... "

"I ... ."

Crossing a street. Moving on, away from home.

"I walked out on her. More than thirty years ago. She wasn't much older than Shelley is now. Little bit.

"Old enough to remember me. Young enough I was her 'mommy.'"

Arnold stopped to sniff at a spot where he always stopped to sniff. Apparently satisfied that it smelled the way it always smelled, the way it was supposed to smell, he moved on.

Yvonne, now heading toward them, flipped a cigarette butt into the street. Arnold recognized it as non-food. "Oh, Debra, we probably can't even have a lot of people at the funeral. Some new size limits," she said.

Debra nodded, her face showing concern—based on Yvonne's look and tone of voice—but she had no idea what the woman was talking about.

Yes, her mother. But?

"I'm so sorry," Debra said.

Yvonne continued to talk but Debra's mind wandered.

The woman had met Miriam. Did she now somehow know who she was or about Emily or Shelley or the guys moving the car or ...

" ... glad at least she doesn't have to go through it," Yvonne said.

"Yes."

Yvonne let out a big breath. Straightened up. And said, "Thank you so much for listening."

"Of course."

"Good morning, Arnold!"

Head up. No food. Head down.

"I better get back to the house," Yvonne said. "My sister ... Arghhh! Bleah." A rolling of her eyes. "I mean I love her. I really do. But ... family! Drama, drama, drama. You know?"

Debra knew.

The women hugged, said their goodbyes, and each turned toward her home. Debra thinking about the encounter.

"Vonnie's always been a little … kooky," she said.

Arnold: Head up and looking back in less than an instant. Eyes fixed on Debra. Laser beams.

"What the … ? You big dumb goof. I said 'kooky.'"

Arnold nodding in agreement.

"Oh, for God's sake. At home. At home."

The dog picked up the pace, forcing Debra to do the same. The leash between them taut.

Maybe it's all a dream, Debra tried again. The whole shebang.

No Miriam.

No Shelley.

No car.

No sick woman, no Emily.

No such luck. Was it bad luck?

They hustled along, Debra lost in thought until she noticed the car. *The* car.

Still parked next to Debra's front fence.

Parallel to it.

"Oh, God. Oh, God. Oh, God."

Miriam and Shelley were on the front porch. They spotted Arnold and Debra and then both the sixty-plus-year-old and the four-year-old began to twirl their right arms like a windmill blade.

And laugh and laugh.

Debra let go of the leash and Arnold shot forward.

"Hell of a dream," she said. "No dream. "Hell."

30

Shelley ran down the steps and out to the gate. As soon as she had it unlatched Arnold rushed in, circled her twice, and then jumped up so his front paws were on her shoulders. Both fell to the ground. Little-girl giggles and squeals; old-dog barks and *rarrrs*.

At the same time Miriam pretended to let something sail from her still-rotating arm and watch it rise high into the air and then fall. Landing on the top of Debra's head.

Splat!

The thought, the insight, hit Debra. She *wanted* this to be real. Her daughter! Her granddaughter! What had she been thinking? Of course she wanted this to be real!

A real mess.

A wonderful mess.

A God-given mess.

My little girl is asleep in my bed.

A miracle.

In the how-many days since Miriam had shown up—appeared?— how many miracles have I seen?

Her dog and her granddaughter got to their feet. Neither seemed to care that the grass had been damp. And probably cold, too.

"I'm just going to let it be," Debra yelled to Miriam.

"There you go," she answered.

"It's good to have Mother Mary come to me."

"Well, aren't you sweet."

Now Debra at the foot of the porch steps, Miriam still on the porch.

"What did you hit me with?" Debra said.

"Me? No, no, no."

"Someone did."

"It happens."

What had happened? Debra thought about that for a few moments. "A moment of clarity," she said.

"Uh huh."

"You did that."

"Nah. Not I."

"Who?"

"The Master of Surprises."

"Who?" Or was it "what"?

"The Paraclete," Miriam said. "The Holy Spirit. Don't get me started!"

Then from Shelley: "Who has a parakeet?"

"Little-child hearing abilities," Miriam said.

"Mrs. Sparger had a parakeet," Shelley said, walking up next to Debra.

"Who?" said Debra, realizing she was getting in a bit of rut here.

"Mrs. Sparger. She lived by us in another 'partment."

"Ah," Miriam said. "What color was it?"

"Her 'partment?"

"Her parakeet."

"Oh. Green. And blue." Pause. Thinking. "And white."

"Multicolored," Debra said.

"What's that?"

"More than one color."

"Oh." More thought.

"But not mixed into one color," Debra said. " Part one color and part another." She stopped short of adding "each retaining its own particular color."

"Okay."

"And some colors mix together to make another color," Miriam said. "Like red and yellow make orange."

"Oranges!"

"No. The color orange."

"Oh."

Child and dog were listening carefully. One because this was a little interesting, the other because perhaps one of the big things would say "cookie" and this time mean it.

"Maybe we can paint some pictures today," Debra said, assuming Miriam would "find" a kid's paint set in the house somewhere. "Mix some colors together. Red and blue make purple."

"I like pink," Shelley said.

"Red and white make pink," Debra said.

Shelley was looking at the backs of her hands. Thinking.

"Black and white make me. *Mon père et mes mères. Papa and Mommy.* "

"Oui," Miriam said. Très bon."

"Merci."

"Tu es très bon!"

"Merci beaucoup et toi aussi."

Debra was lost. Arnold, too, but he looked comfortable with the situation.

"We're just telling each other that we're good," Miriam said.

"Et grand-mère aussi," Shelley said.

"And grandma, too," Miriam translated.

Debra took two deep breaths.

"Mercy," she whispered. "Lord, have mercy."

31

Forty-five minutes later Debra sat on the couch in her living room. Amazed at how long, and packed, the day had been. Stretching back to Shelley tapping on the front door.

Maybe Miriam did that. Stretched time. It wouldn't have surprised her.

It hadn't been even twenty-four hours?

Arnold shifted his head. On her lap. The rest of him splayed out down the sofa. The classic movie channel on TV. Fred and Ginger doing what Fred and Ginger were known for.

"A simpler time," Debra said, but realizing that wasn't true. "There are no simpler times. Every time, all the time, has its share of shhtuff."

An attempt to curb her language now with a preschooler in the house.

Arnold started to snore.

Miriam and Shelley were upstairs, making noise, moving things, talking, laughing.

"'Grandma Mim.' Hell of a lot better than … "

Curbing how one spoke wasn't all that easy. Frustrating.

"God damn it!" A little too loudly.

Silence upstairs.

"Sorry," she yelled toward the stairs. Then, whispering: "Crap, I'm gonna wake Emmy."

Silence downstairs.

Okay. Something else. Think about something else. Fred and Ginger glided.

She scratched Arnold behind his left ear. He sighed his appreciation without waking.

"Sure, they screw up, the director yells 'cut,' and they get to fix it. Nothing shows. No one knows."

Screw up.

Booze.

Drugs.

Infidelity.

Abandonment. A husband and a little girl. *Her* husband. *Her* little girl.

"Mommy."

"Gramma Debby."

"Bullsh ... "

She clamped her hand over her mouth. *Language! The harder I try the worse I get.*

Or maybe she had spoken that way for the last quarter of a century and hadn't noticed. No one *to* notice.

No one.

"Like to see a blooper reel," she said to Arnold. "Fred and Ginger outtakes." She nodded, liking the idea.

Her personal "blooper reel" began spinning in her mind. Going faster and faster. Daughter, husband, words, booze, drugs, bars, motels, men with blurred faces, years, decades.

Again her hand clamping over her mouth. Teeth clenched.

One scene. Picking up the phone. An unknown voice. Her parents. An accident ...

"Stop, stop, stop," she whispered, hand still over mouth, teeth still clenched.

"Please, God, make it stop. Please, God, I don't know what the hell I'm doing or what's going on. Please."

"Come see," Miriam softly shouted from the second floor. *Softly shouted?* A woman of many, many talents.

"We did some stuff," Shelley added.

I did some stuff.

Real stuff.

Really bad stuff.

She clicked the remote. Frederick Austerlitz and Virginia McMath disappeared.

32

Debra saw the "stuff" Miriam and Shelley had done. Several piles of ... items ... were crowding the hallway. The little bedroom was bigger than she remembered it ever being Not huge, but lovely.

"Mim said maybe some junk could go in the basement," Shelley said, proud of what the two of them had accomplished. "Now my room has more room"

My room?

But of course "my room." She and Emmy would have to stay for a while. Till they were back on their feet. Not days. Probably weeks. Couple of months.

And then? Then they would be on their way.

The thought made Debra give a one-note whimper. Surprising her, Shelley, and Arnold—now the room-revitalizing supervisor.

""You're over there in your room," Shelley continued, pointing toward the other upstairs bedroom. "And Mommy is downstairs until she's better. Mim says it would be hard for her to climb stairs and I can't sleep in her bed when she's sick. Mim says she has the flu or something."

Oh. Dear. God. In. Heaven.

Or something.
Or something.
Or something.
Stupid, stupid, stupid.
How could she be so stupid?

"She says you know how to sew," Shelley said and Debra nodded. "Will you teach me?"

Another nod, then: "Of course, honey."

"We'll make masks."

How in holy hell have I not given a single thought to …

"You have lots of pretty … " Shelley looked at Miriam

"Fabric," Miriam said.

"I like the pink ones," Shelley said.

"Me, too," from Debra.

"Can we make a shirt for me?"

Nod.

"Like the mask. I mean both pink."

Nod.

"Are you okay, Gramma?"

"Older women can have so much on their minds," Miriam told her. "Sometimes dealing with something new and kind of forgetting about something else."

"How could I have … " from Debra. More to herself than to Miriam.

"Slipped your mind," Miriam said.

"That's not possible."

Miriam shrugged. "And yet … "

"Impossible!"

"Visit from me, estranged daughter, unknown granddaughter."

"Wear a mask, wash your hands, stay … I forget," Shelley said.

"Six feet apart," Debra and Miriam said.

"How big is six feet?" Shelly asked and Miriam touched a spot on the wall.

"So somebody has to be up there?"

Two smiles.

Miriam stepped six feet away from the pair. "This far."

"Oh."

Shelley gave Debra a "grown-up" look that said "I know things."

"It's because of the … " A little scowl. "I forget."

"Virus," Debra said. "I forgot, too.

"Mim says it makes you very tired and you cough a lot and you get a fever."

Debra grabbed a fabric swatch and was out the door and down the stairs.

33

Emily was asleep, breathing heavily. Debra had one hand holding a folded square of cloth that was clamped against her own nose and mouth. She reached forward and gently placed the other hand on her daughter's forehead.

No, no, no. God, no, no, no.

The fastest, deepest, most sincere pray of her life.

Then a sigh.

Oh, thank you, thank you, thank you!

A coolness a mother doesn't forget. Yes, you have a fever. No, you don't.

"No, you don't." Muffled behind the cloth, but still loud.

"Mom?" Eyes closed. A whisper.

"You keep resting, honey."

Eyes half open. "Is Shelley okay?"

"She's fine."

"Did she get my cough?"

"She's fine. No cough. Full of energy."

"I'm so tired."

"You rest. Do you want some chicken soup?"

"With lotsa balls," Emily said gently.

"With lotsa balls."

"Isn't Shelley beautiful?"

"Perfect."

"Rochelle."

"What?"

"Shelley. Rochelle. I named her after Grandma."

Another brief whimper.

"You remember Grandma?"

"Little bit. And Grandpa."

Tears spilled from Debra's eyes.

"I'm so sorry I ... " she began but her child's eyes had closed.

She rested her hand on the forehead one more time.

Still cool.

34

Evening. Miriam and Shelley in the basement doing laundry. Sheets and pillow cases and blankets and bedspreads. Debra and Arnold on the sofa. Watching TV. No, looking toward the TV. A show about sort-of-famous people dressed like cartoon animals or creatures and singing.

As usual, Arnold's head resting in Debra's lap. Half asleep. Debra in a half daze. Trying to sort out how a pandemic was affecting her life.

The diner open.

No masks among the locals.

No news or gossip about someone she knew who had come down with the virus. Dire warnings and predictions but somehow never hitting home.

Up there, on the other side of Seattle.

Over there, in China or Italy.

Not in Black Diamond.

Probably all settle down in a few weeks. The medical or science or whoever people will figure out how to treat it and how to make a vaccine to protect everyone and ... .

A little inconvenience for now.

Emily with an old fashioned flu or cold. Rest up. Eat right.

Good as new.

Except …

"I don't know the new Emily. When I left, faded, tumbled, ran away, she was the old Emily. The old young Emily. Now the new old Emily."

No fever.

Debra clung to that like a …

"Like a what?"

Arnold stirred.

"These were in Mommy's car." Shelley. Up from the basement. "Mim and I went out and got them. Did you know there's a door down there that goes outside? Two large photo albums in her arms. "Mommy was a little girl."

She dumped the load on Debra's lap, on Arnold's head. The dog gave startled "*Rurrr?*" and scooted back toward the far end of the sofa.

"Oh, sorry!"

"He's fine."

Shelley plopped down into his former spot and opened the cover of the top album. "Mommy was a little girl," she said. "Mim told me some who was who. You looked like Mommy."

Debra was silent.

"And Mim says this is Mommy's daddy. Did she call him '*mon père*' or 'Papa'?"

Debra shook her head. Still unable to speak. Shelley looked up at her.

"No."

Shelley waited.

"She called him 'Daddy.'"

"Oh." She turned to the next page. A thought. Not looking up. "And I call you 'Gramma Debby' and I called him 'Grampa Mike.'"

"You … "

'Called'? Past tense?

"So … you don't see Grampa Mike anymore?"

"No." Still absorbed in the snapshots. "He passed away last summer." Then looking up at Debra. "That means he went up to heaven."

What was that Tom Cruise movie where he says, "And the hits just keep on coming"?

"That's sad," Debra managed.

"Mommy was sad. She cried a lot. Then Papa got ported—deee-ported— and she cried then, too. And I cried. And Mommy said 2019 is a poopy year only she didn't say 'poopy' and she said 2020 is going to be a lot better."

35

A Few Good Men. That was the movie. She remembered the title and the line but nothing else from it. Didn't matter. Lights out, in her "new" bedroom. Arnold, fast asleep, hogging the bed. She gave him a shove and he fell on the floor by the wall. Grunted but didn't wake up. Or stop snoring.

"Victory." Under her breath.

"Who was that guy?" She looked up at the ceiling. "Dealt the bad hand. In the Bible."

God, whom she was addressing, didn't answer.

"You know." Trying to remember. "Royally shafted. Doesn't matter."

A pause.

"So what's your deal?"

Punishment came to mind. On her and on her daughter and granddaughter. The sins of a mother being slapped on descendants.

Arnold broke wind.

"Oh, for the love of ... "

The smell reached its way up to the bed.

"Oh, *really,* for the love of ... "

She used the edge of a pillowcase to cover her nose and

mouth. "COVID-*20,* release of the Arnold gas." Rather pleased with her joke.

But her concerns, like a darkness, edged their ways back into her thoughts

When Emmy gets better will she leave me just like I left her?

And take Shelley.

The two of them. A second chance? A do-over? Or a punishment. See what you could have had? Could have right now?

Whoosh. Gone.

Well, you don't have that. You're alone. Now and forever. Some Bible quote about sowing and reaping.

And Miriam. A Godsend. Ha! But, at some point, she'd leave, too.

Arnold. Old. Maybe another "incident." Maybe the next time …

Get tough, Debra. You are *tough. You made it for how many years on your own and now when you've got something really good happening you're focusing on, obsessing on …*

Look, you dumb old lady! Look at what you have right here, right now.

Your daughter.

Your granddaughter.

And the freaking mother of God.

Under your roof. Now.

In your life. Now.

The bedroom door opened just a little. A tiny voice. "I had a scary dream." An automatic response. Covers tossed back. Occupant scooting over.

"It's okay. Come on."

36

On a Friday afternoon in early October, fourth-grader Debra Patrick stole a classmate's plastic stencil ruler.

Red. Twelve inches.

It was so neat! It had punched-out letters and numbers. With a little effort you could write your name or anything else you wanted and it looked really neat.

"Neat" was very important in the fourth grade.

No, she didn't really steal it. For some reason she had found herself alone in the classroom and saw a red plastic stencil ruler on the floor and she picked it up and slid it into her desk. Thought better of that—"better" meaning more slyly not more virtuously—and hid it in the bottom of her book bag.

Not stealing. Finding. On the floor. Under the desk of a classmate who had a red plastic stencil ruler.

But!

No name on the ruler. Debra had checked.

She took it home and played with it in her bedroom. Alone. Being an only child had its advantages.

With a piece of light blue construction paper, a pencil with a very sharp point, and her red plastic stencil ruler she printed out:

DEBRA T PATRICK and AGE 9 and PHONE NUMBER LAKEVIEW 2-5573.

Excited at the excellent job she had done—it looked so neat!—she rushed out to show her mother. Nine-year-olds are not known for their ability to think things through.

Her mother confiscated the ruler and told young Debra, in no uncertain terms, that she was going to return it to her classmate first thing Monday morning *and* she was going to go to confession tomorrow.

Tomorrow!

Now, no one can *make* you say what they want you to say in the confessional of a Roman Catholic church, but a mother *can* tell if you did what you were told to do. Or not.

Brush your teeth. Take out the garbage. Clean your room. Confess being a thief.

Father Kowalski was cool about it. A word Debra would come to embrace only a few years later. It replacing "neat." She realized he was cool about it even before appreciating the concept of "cool."

She spilled the beans, throwing herself on the mercy of Jesus Christ and Father Kowalski. It seemed both were of the opinion of "small harm, small foul" and give the ruler back to the owner.

Make an Act of Contrition now.

Say a Hail Mary once you leave the confessional.

Go in peace.

Awesome! (Again, not a term Debra knew or used when she was nine. And knew, but didn't use, when she was sixty-five.)

Completely forgiven! Such a relief.

So, first thing Monday morning, out on the playground/parking lot, she pulled the ruler out of her book bag, handed it to its rightful owner, and apologized.

The owner punched her in the chest.

It hurt. It really hurt.

But … but … but …

A lesson here.

Two lessons.

One: Hell hath no fury like a fourth-grade girl whose read plastic stencil ruler you have stolen.

And two: Confession cleans up your soul but it doesn't do the same for what's happening elsewhere. The temporal effects, the ramifications, of what you've done or failed to do.

Again, Debra had no clue of such concepts or language back then.

But she did now. In 2020, with her daughter. The then-little girl she had abandoned so long ago.

37

Debra awoke with that story, that part of her history, on her mind. Not that she had dreamed about it, just—*bam!*—it was there. Rebuilding a relationship with Emily was more than simply "mending fences." A lot more. And she had no clue how or when to begin.

Shelley was up and gone. Arnold, too. Debra could hear both of them in Shelley's room.

"Shhh! You'll wake Gramma!"

"*Rurr, rarrr, rurr, rurr.*"

"That what I said."

Footsteps coming up the stairs. A door opening. "Okay. Come on." Miriam. "Quiet as mice."

Footsteps and paw-steps down the stairs.

Then Debra's maternal instincts, still rusty and uncertain, sparked. Up quickly and dressed. A pressing need to see her daughter. To check on her.

No fever yesterday. But now?

38

Emily was sleeping. Seemed to be breathing well. No fever. How Debra loved that diagnosis after putting her hand on that forehead.

She stepped back out of the room and went to the kitchen. "No fever," she said.

Miriam gave her a thumbs up. Shelley saw her do that and imitated it.

"Are you hungry?" Miriam asked and Debra shrugged, thought about it, then nodded.

"Scrambled eggs?"

Another nod. "Thank you."

"Can I help?" This from Shelley.

"Someone needs to beat the eggs," Miriam said.

"I can do that till they're black and blue," the four-year-old said and both women laughed.

"Where'd you learn that?" Debra asked and Shelley shrugged.

"Just beat them till they're all mixed up and frothy."

"Frosty?"

"Frothy. Kind of foamy."

A blank look.

"Miriam will tell you when to stop," Debra said.

"What are you going to do?" Shelley asked.

"Sit down, drink coffee, and kibbitz."

The Blessed Virgin Mary laughed. Then to Shelley. "Oy vey, your bubbe ... and a *gentile*. What are we going to do with her?"

"I don't know what you're saying."

"Yiddish. A language," Miriam said, "with Jewish roots."

"Can you teach me?"

"Of course. Such a mensch."

Shelley *and* Debra looked blank.

"You are a wonderful, wonderful, wonderful, dear little one. And you, bubbe, Gramma Debby, are an honorable woman."

Shelley looked pleased; Debra on the verge of tears, shaking her head "no."

"Yes," Miriam said. "Would I lie?"

"But ... "

"We all have 'buts'," she said and Shelley laughed.

"We all have butts," she mimicked and patted herself on her bottom.

"Let me rephrase that," Miriam said, giving Shelley a playful smack on the back of her head. "Such language from a little lady. We all have reasons, sometimes lots of them, to say—and believe— 'but I did this and this and this and so I am *not* good.'"

Debra looked at her.

"No one is perfect," Miriam said and Debra raised her eyebrows. "For the sake of this discussion, let's say no one is perfect."

"Okay."

"But most people are good."

Eyebrows raised again.

"Ups and downs, ups and downs, sometimes far and frequent downs but ... " quickly and gently taking Shelley's hand before there could be any bottom-patting ... "up and up and up is possible. Seldom if ever one gigantic up. Tiny up after tiny up after tiny up. Like … "

"Baby steps," Shelley said, astounding both women.

"Sharp as a tack," Miriam said.

"No flies on her," Debra said.

"So can we cook eggs now?" Shelley asked. "Can I open them up?"

39

It amazed the two old woman—old through a four-year-old's eyes and sometimes old through their own when staring into a mirror under fluorescent lighting— how easily a child adapts.

Mommy is sick in that room. My room is upstairs next to a grandmother's I just met. My friend Mim sleeps in the basement. And Arnold is all over the place.

Now she knew how to make soup and scrambled eggs and maybe today sew a face mask.

A pink one.

But first, go see Mommy and find out if she would like eggs and toast. And maybe jam or marmalade.

"Or both?" she asked.

"Sure," Debra said. "We can go ask her."

Again with the sneaking and peeking because, well, because that was how it was done. Plus it was fun. For Shelley. For Debra. For Miriam. For Arnold. First, second, third, and fourth in line. Shelley stopping at the bedroom's nearly-closed door, turning back, giving the universal sign for "shhh" and then taking a look inside.

"Mommy!" And in.

The ladies gave them some time alone. The dog didn't.

"It's been a long while since I played with a preschooler," Debra said.

"Happy memories," Miriam said. "Little Jay. He could be a handful. On the *go!*"

"Emmy wanted to learn the rules and then make sure everyone followed them."

"Liked to be in charge?"

"No, more wanted it to be fair. The ultimate complaint that fit countless occasions. "It's not fair!""

Miriam smiled. "And then discovering, beyond a doubt, life isn't fair."

"There was a country song a few years back that pointed out sometimes you're the windshield and sometimes you're the bug."

"I remember that," Miriam said. "It was a good one."

"You remember everything? No. Wait. Don't tell me. It's part of that very large list of 'things you can't understand.'"

"Right now."

"Right now," Debra said. "Maybe later?"

"Maybe. Or maybe later you won't care about things like that."

"After I'm dead."

"Yes."

"What if I hadn't beaned you with poop and had just stayed inside the house that day?"

"I'd have kicked in your front door." Giving a half-hearted demonstration with a well-worn moon-gray running shoe.

"You don't lie."

"But I do joke."

"That's fair."

They could hear Shelley filling in her mother on many, many things. Right now, the guys—"Mim's friends"—who had moved their car. And how yesterday she and Mim had gotten the photo albums out of the car and she had looked at some pictures with Gramma Debby.

Emily laughed at the name and then that slid into a series of deep coughs.

"Is she … " Concern on Debra's face.

"It's a cold," Miriam said, patting her on the shoulder. "Really."

"Really?"

"I have it on the highest authority."

"So … ." Miriam waited. "So nothing like Mrs. McConkey."

"No, Debra. Nothing like that. She didn't have, and Emily doesn't have, COVID."

"You're sure. I mean really sure, no screwing around here."

"Yes. Your knowing that is a gift from me to you."

Debra gave her one of the biggest hugs she had ever given in her entire life.

"Thank you, thank you, thank you." She pulled back, then: "You're really sure?" and Miriam nodded.

She held up the first three fingers, side by side, of her right hand. "Holy Trinity's honor."

"I thought you were going to say 'scouts.'"

"First time I ever did that little pledge/promise."

"Yeah?"

"You're breaking new ground with me here. So … why not?" She hooked one of her little fingers into one of Debra's. "Pinky swear."

Shelley bounced out of the bedroom. As did Arnold. "Mommy says toast and eggs and I can decide jam or the other thing. And tea."

"She's feeling a little better," Miriam said.

"It was the soup," Shelley said.

"She told you that?"

"I just know."

"We'll bring the meal," Miriam said to Debra. "Why don't you grab a chair and go on in and visit?"

40

Still coming off her it's-not-COVID-19 high, Debra did what Miriam had suggested. Now seated beside the bed in a dining room chair, facing her daughter.

Facing the music.

"Thank you, Mom," Emily began, half sitting up against the headboard.

Thank you?

"For what?" Truly puzzled.

"Taking care of Shelley. You and your friend."

"Oh … all of us are having a good time."

Which seemed a strange thing to say, considering the circumstances. What were the circumstances? Debra's child—Emmy—abandoned. Now here in Debra's bed.

Debra stared at the floor and the silence became awkward. "Mom?" No response. "Mom?"

"Yes." Glancing up then looking back down.

"I have a question."

It felt as if every muscle in Debra's body tightened.

Then: "What's the deal with that monstrosity they're building next door? Practically in your house."

"Yes!" Now looking up. Making and maintaining eye

contact. "Monstrosity. Exactly!"

"Did they tear down an old house?"

"No! It was a lovely, vacant, small, odd-shaped gone-to-seed-years-ago empty lot. Forever."

"I heard workers so I looked out the living room window."

"You walked that far? You could have fallen."

"My big adventure yesterday morning. Yesterday? Anyway."

"I thought you weren't walking any farther than the bathroom."

"I felt brave. And I had to find out. The bedroom window only shows a wall. The living room window shows it is U-G-L-Y."

"It *is*."

Both women smiled. Common ground. A good thing.

Then, from Debra: "Shelley is an angel."

"Wel-l-l-l-l ... "

"You know what I mean. A really good little girl. Quick."

"She gets a lot of that from her dad."

"And a lot of it from her mom. I'm sure of that."

"Thank you."

"Parenting isn't easy."

Lightly touching a live wire. Backing away.

Emily navigating smoothly. "So tell me about Miriam. Mim. She's a friend of yours?"

"A longtime friend," Debra said, swallowing an added "that I met a few days ago."

She *had* met her a few days ago. And she *was* a longtime friend.

The Lord works in convoluted ways.

Debra told her how their paths had crossed, recrossed, outside the monstrosity.

"You hit her in the head with a bag of poop!"

"Barely. Glanced right off."

"That's a great story."

"She's really something." For some unknown reason not getting into what Church scholars refer to as Theotokos, the Mother of God. Not that Debra had ever heard the term.

If I don't get it how can I explain it? Other than both she and I being whacko.

"Shelley is quite taken with her. 'Mim.' And you. 'Gramma Debby.'"

Arnold shot through the doorway and bounded up on the bed.

"God da ... "

"It's okay," Emily said. Then, with hands on both sides of the dog's head: "You big, dumb dog."

"*Rurr, rurr, rarr, rurr, rurr.*"

"Uh huh. I know. Bet I stole your spot, huh?"

"*Rurr.*"

Shelley at the door, carefully using both little hands to carry a plate of scrambled eggs and toast. "Made with a secret in-gree-da-dent." A pause. "Love."

After Arnold had been banished from the room and Emily—with Shelley seated next to her—had nibbled on the food and sipped a bit of the tea Miriam had brought her, it became obvious fatigue was settling in on her.

"Mommy needs a nap," Debra said, reaching out a hand toward Shelley.

"Okay, Mommy," Emily said taking Debra's hand. "I thought I was too old for naps."

"You gotta eat and you gotta sleep," Shelley said, startling Debra.

A phrase, a lesson, she had come up with and used with little Emmy. Now passed down to the next generation.

She looked at Miriam who nodded.

41

As they tiptoed from the room—Shelley again demonstrating for Emily how that was done—Debra glanced at her watch and was surprised to see an hour had passed. A good hour. And she was not surprised to see that Arnold, no tiptoe-er, was ready to go outside. Shelley, too, who took the plate back to the kitchen and then hopped, skipped, jumped to the front door and grabbed Arnold's leash.

"Walkies," Debra said.

"What's that?"

"Taking a dog for a walk."

"Oh. Yeah. Walkies!"

"The queen of England was one to say that. Or it's reported she said that."

"Does she live near here?"

"No. I saw her say it on TV."

"Oh." Shelley snapped the leash onto Arnold's collar, who jumped up and knocked her over.

"Get your coat, honey, and I'll get mine."

"And a hat," Shelley said.

"And a hat."

"You need a hat and coat," Shelley shouted toward the

kitchen.

"You three go," Miriam answered. "I'll just putter around here."

"Okay." A pause. "What's 'putter'?"

"Do a bunch of little things," Miriam said.

"Okay. Putter butter."

"Putter butter."

Then out the door, down the steps, through the gate, and a turn to the left.

"That's our car," Shelley said, pointing as if Debra might not see the vehicle parked in front of her house or know whose it was.

"It's a nice one," Debra said, not technically a lie even though it was old and pretty beat up. *But then, so am I.*

They continued walking.

"Did you see Mim's friends move it?"

"I did. They woke me up."

"Me, too. They were loud."

"Yes, they were."

"Mim said we were lucky Gabey didn't honk the horn."

"Gabey?"

"One of the guys."

"Uh huh."

"Mikey drove and Gabey and Rafey helped."

"I see."

"They were funny. Gabey and Rafey. Mikey was ... ." Searching for a word or phrase.

"All business," Debra said.

"What's that mean?"

"Not playing around."

"Mikey was all business. Where are we going?" Passing the under-construction house.

"Up by the school."

"Okay."

Arnold stopped suddenly and sniffed the base of a power pole with great concentration. The other two waited until he was ready to move on.

"I'm going to go to school this year," Shelley said.

"When's your birthday?"

Guilt! Debra didn't know it.

"July seven. I'll be five." Four fingers and a thumb spread out and held up to her grandmother.

"A big girl," Debra said.

"Kinda." Thinking. "How many are you?"

Debra did the same with one hand.

"You're not five!"

"Wait. Hold the leash." Then flashing all thumbs and fingers on both hands six times and then adding one hand's worth.

"You're old. Is the walkies lady old like you?"

Much older but ... yes.

"Yes."

"Is it much farther to this school?"

"A little bit. It has a playground."

Shelley nodded. "So does my school. Back home. I'm going to kindee-garden."

Arnold stopped again, this time sniffing familiar territory. He had several routes and on each, *the* places for urination and defecation.

This, Debra knew, was a poop place.

"He's all business when he does his business," Shelley observed. Then making a face and handing the leash back to Debra.

How Debra loved this little girl. How she would miss ...

Stop it!

42

Arnold walked the two-legged things home and then, tuckered out, made it up the front steps, stumbled inside, and scrambled-up-lay-down on the sofa. Sighed twice and began to snore. Shelley looked in on her mom—still sleeping—and then joined Arnold, resting head to head.

"Here," Debra said, putting an afghan over her. "You take a little rest."

"Uh huh." Already past half asleep.

"I'm going out for a little bit. Mim is here."

No response.

And from the kitchen doorway, Miriam whispered: "I'll keep an eye on them. Later, Shelley can help me make bagels."

"Bagels were around in the first century?"

"My people have been coming up with new menu items for millennia."

"Thank you." A nod toward Shelley.

"My absolute pleasure."

The truth was Debra was finding it a little … challenging having so many guests in her house. Glad to have them but not used to others being there. Just Arnold and her. And even then the mutt could get on her nerves sometimes.

"You have to go out *right now*? It's … four in the morning. Dumb dog."

Now, through the first quarter mile, she tried to think of nothing. Impossible.

Miriam. Shelley. Emily.

Miriam: Well, apparently you could get used to anything. Anyone. And, Debra had to admit, she was maybe the perfect houseguest.

Shelley: The best surprise of her life. Out of the blue. Or, rather, out of the dark of night. That sweet, sweet—and brilliant—child. But, well, tiring.

Emily: Uh oh.

Yes, having her come back into Debra's life was another "best surprise." Emily and little Shelley.

So what was the problem?

"So what's the problem?" she said out loud. Considered it.

Now at half a mile.

Debra knew the problem. Debra was the problem. All those years ago, what she did and didn't do, that was the problem. No time machine. No live and let live. No …

No way to keep Emily here, keep her and Shelley here— meaning wanting them to stay here, close by—after the conversation turns to "What a crappy mother you were! You ruined me!"

Or some such.

It would. The truth would come out. She had no defense. No excuses. Not really any good reasons.

Why did I do that? What was, what is, wrong with me?

Maybe it would happen again. At some point, not leave them, but give them the boot. Tell them to leave.

"Impossible!"

But not.

A jumble of thoughts, none pleasant, till the one-mile

119

mark and then turning around. Heading for home.

First things first. So ... ?

"Get Emmy back to good health."

Right. And that could take days or even weeks. In the meantime ... what?

"Follow her lead."

What lead? Keep the conversation, keep the topics, light. Common ground. The house being built next door is a complete eyesore. Shelley is wonderful. Matzo ball soup is good.

"Things like that."

It could work. For a time.

She picked up the pace.

Bagels.

"Bagels."

She assumed Miriam would "find" some cream cheese in the back of the refrigerator.

Help Emily get better and keep it light.

A plan. For now.

43

Debra was no fireball when it came to walking but she could cover two miles round-trip in forty-five minutes. By then dog and child were up watching something on television. A program aimed at kids. Singing and silliness. Lot of colors, probably with some subliminal message and lesson on kindness or climate change or whatever.

"I punched it," Shelley said as Debra hung up her coat in the front closet. "Real hard." She smacked her right fist into her left palm.

"Wham!"

"The dough," Miriam said from the kitchen.

"Yeah. The dough. Have you ever punched the dough?"

"I have," Debra said.

"It feels good."

"It does."

"The next time you can watch me when I punch it," Shelley said.

"Okay."

"When you make bay-gals you punch the dough and then you make them into doughnuts but not doughnuts and let them rest and then give them a bath and put them in the oven."

"Oh?"

"Yeah. You never made bay-gals?"

"No."

"Oh." A pause, thinking that over. "Me and Mim ..."

"'Mim and I,'" Debra said automatically.

"Yeah, Mim and I will teach you how."

"I look forward to it."

"Me, too."

"Did you have a good little nap."

"Yeah. But ... ."

"Yes?"

"Arnold."

"What about Arnold?"

"He ... he made smelly."

Debra took a moment to translate, decided not to mention "flatulence."

"He does that sometimes."

"You think Mommy will like bay-gals?"

"Yes."

"Me, too. I think she will lu-u-u-u-v-v-v-v-v them."

"I think she will."

"Good."

Yes, good. Something else to talk about. Something safe.

"Is Mommy still sleeping?" Debra asked.

"Uh huh."

"That's good. She needs her rest."

"To get better."

"Yes."

"All better." A glance at the television show. Then: "Can we ... " Pointing upstairs. Shelley seeing that Gramma Debby wasn't getting it. "You know. With the thing." Nothing. "The thing that makes the things." A blank. Shelley put her hand over her own mouth and nose. "And a shirt." Muffled.

"Sew," Debra said.

"So what!" Shelley said, dropping her hand and really

liking her joke.

Debra smiled. "That's a good one."

"So can we sew?"

"Sure. You're going to love the pinking shears."

"What's a 'shears'?"

"A scissors."

Shelley's mouth dropped open. Her eyes went wide. "A scissors *just* for pink!"

God, how Debra loved this child.

44

The world looks different through a young child's eyes. The world *is* different. One filled with magic and wonder and surprise. Yes, there's the possibility of a monster under the bed but someone older, someone wiser, someone stronger is on hand to offer assurances.

"It's all right. You're all right."

Except when it isn't. Except when you aren't.

Now, with bits and bobs of sewing items spread out on the bed—including five pieces of fabric each with a different shade of pink—Shelley was beaming and chattering and asking and it couldn't have been better. Couldn't.

For her.

But not for Debra and she didn't know why. Something was wrong. A whiff of "something under the bed." A chill, not in the air, but in her.

Probably, she decided, subconsciously anticipating the day when Shelley would leave. Emmy would leave. Debra would be abandoned. Just as she had abandoned Emily.

No, it wasn't the same. Debra wasn't just a child. It wasn't *her mother* who had walked out.

Stumbled out.

Gone away.

Stayed away.

What. In. The. Hell!

With Shelley's and her own thumb and index and middle fingers in the scissors' fingers holes, a child learned and an adult taught how pinking shears are used. And the amazing results of each snip.

A piece of cloth divided into two, each with a serrated edge.

Magic. Wonder. Surprise.

Monster.

The monster had got her. Not the child. The woman.

No, not the woman. A child. A teen. No, child.

The reality, the truth, hit Debra so hard she gasped.

"You okay, Gramma?"

"Oh, I'm fine, honey."

"This is my favorite pink."

"Uh huh."

"No. Wait. This one. No. These two."

"Uh huh."

"Three. These three."

"It's okay to like them all."

"I *love* them all."

"That's okay, too."

"What was that word you used?"

"What word?"

"Yeah. What word?"

"A word for what, honey?"

"All these." A little hand waving over the variety of swatches and folded yards, feet, and inches of cloth.

"Cloth?" Debra asked.

"No. the other one."

The other one? Got it!

"Fabric."

"Yeah. Fabric. With different ... what did you say?"

Debra was clueless.

"What was I talking about when I said it?" she asked.

"Cloth. Um. Fab-brick."

"Uh huh. What about it?"

"They don't all look the same even if they're the same color." Now tugging on the edge of a swatch. Goofing around. Experimenting. Learning.

"Oh, honey, Gramma doesn't remem ... weave?"

"Yeah. Watch."

A light blue square, perhaps eight inches by eight inches. A thick weave with a single fat thread about a quarter of the way from one edge sticking out from the others. A gentle tug by Shelley and it was out completely.

The little girl looked at the thread. Then held up the cloth and stared at it. Through it.

"Now it has a hole," she said. "A long, skinny hole."

45

Shelley carried a pile of fabric downstairs, Debra the sewing machine. Miriam brought the ironing board up from the basement.

Then she went down and up again, this time with an iron. She got Debra's attention and blew dust off it.

"Uh huh," Debra said. "Permanent press. That's my code."

"Look," Shelley said to Miriam. She pulled a spool of thread from each of her front pants pockets. "Light pink, dark pink."

She set them on the dining room table next to the sewing machine, fabric, and iron. "What color mask to do you want?" she asked Miriam.

"Oooh. So many good choices."

"I'm having two shades of pink with dark pink ..." She pointed at the spools.

"Thread," Debra said.

"Yeah."

"Sounds perfect," Miriam said.

"Gramma wants these." Bright green and dark blue. A rolling of the eyes and shake of the head.

"Go, Seahawks," Debra said.

Another shake. "Papa said American football isn't as good as real football."

"Soccer," Debra said.

"*Real* football."

"And what did Mommy say?"

"'Go, 49ers!'" Arms in the air. A true cheer.

"Ugh," Debra said, partly pretending to be disgusted.

"You?" Shelley asked Miriam.

"I like to root for the home team wherever I am."

"What's a home team?"

"The one right here. Shelley, Mommy, and Gramma Debby."

"And you."

"And me."

"Home team!" Then eyes on Debra. "So … ?"

Debra tossed the blue and green pieces of cloth back onto the pile.

"Go, pink."

"Or you stink," Shelley cheered and gave the ladies a look. Then from Miriam and Debra: "Or you stink."

As Debra wiped down the sewing machine with a dish cloth and set up the ironing board, Shelley and Miriam peeked in on Emily. "Sleeping," Shelley reported. "She's very tired."

"Breathing more easily," Miriam said and Debra gave a sigh of relief.

"Have you noticed? Miriam asked. "Less coughing today."

"On the mend?" Debra asked, unable to keep the hope and concern from her voice.

Shelley, sharp as ever: "What's 'mend'?"

"On the mend. Getting better," Debra said, looking hard at Miriam.

"On the mend."

Debra, softly: "Oh, God. Oh, God. Oh, God."

Shelley, whispering: "Amen."

Surprised when both woman leaned in and kissed her on the top of her head.

A little girl with an enormous smile.

"Go, pink."

Shelley spent the rest of the afternoon dividing her time between sewing, baking, and checking on Mommy. Arnold following her every step of the way, a little annoyed he had yet to taste whatever caused the good smell in the kitchen.

By dinnertime there were three adult-sized masks, one small-child sized mask (based on a pattern that had been online), an oddly home-designed "dog mask" (which quickly became more of a hat), and a plate with a warm bagel for Mommy.

Who, clearly, was very, very impressed.

All were wearing their masks—or hat—and Emily, sitting up in bed, held the plate on her lap.

"Selfie!" Shelley announced. Then to Miriam: "Do you have a cell phone?" A shake of the head. Shelley looking a little surprised.

"Gramma? Never mind. Mommy does."

"In my backpack," Emily said. "I don't know where … "

"I do."

And she was off. On her own. Arnold wasn't straying from the bagel plate.

46

"I'm not coughing as much," Emily said as Debra and Miriam sat down on each side of her with their backs against the headboard.

Shelley in her mother's lap. Arnold stretched out across four sets of human legs. Feeling content, having been fed half of Emily's bagel.

"How about one shot without masks and one with?" Miriam suggested. Four "ayes" and one abstention.

Debra felt her daughter's forehead and smiled.

"I don't want to get you or Miriam sick." Emily said.

"I think you're past the contagious stage," Miriam said. "I'm pretty sure."

"On the mend," Shelley said, fiddling with the phone.

"Were you a nurse?" Emily asked.

"No, just around a lot of sick people over the years."

"Where are you from?"

"Palestine, originally."

"Really!"

"And in Egypt for a little while."

Then from Shelley to Debra, handing her the phone: "Here. *You* take the picture. Make sure you can see all of us and then tap this button."

Debra: Tried. Failed. Even before tapping.

Emily: In the middle, couldn't get the right angle.

Shelley: Bad angle and short arms.

Arnold: No fingers or an opposable thumb.

Miriam: Scooching off the bed, standing, walking to the foot of it. "All right. A family photo. Move in closer. Arnold, look this way."

Dog's head up. Was that thing being held something to eat?

Tap, tap, tap.

"Now," Miriam said, "mask or hat on."

Pink, pink, pink, pink.

Tap, tap, tap.

"And now you," Emily said.

"Maybe later. Come on, little one." And to the dog: "And big, sweet, dumb one. Let's let the two mommies have some time to visit."

Debra's stomach clenched and they were gone.

"I think Miriam knew more about cell phones than she was letting on," Emily said.

"I suspect she had been watching what Shelley had done. Miriam is a fast learner."

"Very bright."

"As the sun."

Still sitting side by side, Emily gave the phone a little shake and said, "Do you want to see some pictures of Samuel?"

"Who?"

"Shelley's dad."

"Oh. I thought he'd have a French name. Haitian."

"It's a popular name there." Emily tapped and swiped and there it was. A different family photo. Two members standing. Emily, holding infant Shelley, and Samuel.

A little older than Emily. Tall. Slender. Dark-skinned. Beautiful white teeth in a glorious smile. A proud papa.

Emily slumped against Debra's shoulder.

131

"Oh, Mom." A tear sliding down her cheek.

"Mom." Not "Mommy." Debra slipped her arm around Emily's shoulders and was clueless.

In less than a few minutes, both were asleep.

47

It was the pain in her shoulder that woke Debra some half hour later. She eased her arm out from under her daughter's head and slowly moved to the side of the bed. Swung her feet over the edge. Stood.

Maybe we won't have to go over what happened back then. Maybe we can start fresh. Just move forward. Just enjoy here and now.

Debra wished it—prayed it—doubted it.

A faint voice from the other side of the house. Little girl. Shelley. Then a laugh-snort. Mother of God. Miriam.

Debra stood watching Emily in the half-light of the doorway. Someone had come in and turned off the lamp on the bedside table.

Emmy. Her little girl. Breathing easily.

"Is Mommy okay?" A whisper. Shelley. Now in the doorway.

"She's doing really well, honey. Come on. Let's let her keep resting."

Then, on the way to the kitchen:

Shelley: "Did you have a good nap?"

Debra: "Very good. I didn't know I was so tired."

Shelley: "You kind of snore."

Debra: "I do?"
Shelley: "Not like Arnold."
Debra: "I would hope not."
Shelley: "Have you ever had green cheese?"
Now at the kitchen. Joining Miriam sitting at the table. Bagels. Sliced apples. Cups of cocoa. Cream cheese.
"You mean have I ever had cream cheese?" Debra asked.
"Yeah."
"Yes."
"It's good."
"It is."
"Here. I'll make you your dinner." Cream cheese applied to the bottom half of a sliced bagel. Liberally. Two slices of apple stuck firmly in it.
"You want cocoa?"
"Sure."
"I'll get it," Miriam said.
Shelley carried the dinner plate around the table and set it in front of Debra. Stood next to her.
"You know what they call this?" she asked. A little index finger pointed so closely and enthusiastically at the cream cheese that it poked it.
"Cream cheese."
"What else?"
Debra shrugged. Miriam set the cup of cocoa next to the plate.
"It's a ... " Looking at Miriam. "I forget."
"Shh," Miriam said.
"I forget," Shelley whispered.
The ladies smiled.
"Repeat after me," Miriam said. "Shh."
"Shh."
"Mmm."
"Mmm."
Miriam touched the side of her head.
Nothing.

Tugged on her ear.

"It's a shhmm-listen. That's not right."

"Shhmm eee … "

"Shhmmm-ear."

"Now say it faster," Miriam. said.

"Schmear. It's a schmear." A smile. Pleased with herself. "That's more Jewish stuff."

"You're learning a lot," Debra said. "Miriam is a good teacher."

"Little Jay was a teacher," Shelley said. "Like Mommy."

"Mommy is a teacher?"

"*Oui.*"

Debra waited.

"French. She taught me. Papa and her taught me."

The women let the grammar slide.

"*Toutes nos félicitations* is the same as *mazel tov,*" Shelley said. "They mean 'Way to go!'"

Debra turned and gave Shelley a hug. "Oh, my goodness," she said. "You're just a little sponge."

Shelley glanced at the sink.

Looking unsure.

48

The next morning. Early. Still dark out.

"What's it called?" Debra asked Arnold who gave no reply. Then she remembered and was okay with it. More than okay. Delighted.

It made her smile. "When was the last time I was delighted?" She thought about that. Probably watching the bag of dog poop rise, pause midair, and then fall.

This was better. Infinitely better. In the single bed in the upstairs bedroom. Shelley and Arnold in the other room. Arnold, who had abandoned her to sleep with Shelley.

No, not abandoned. Took a better offer. Debra didn't blame him. Truth be told, she was sleeping more soundly with the narrow bed entirely to herself and no dog on the floor next to it.

"The new normal."

That was it. The household's new normal. Her new normal.

Different bedroom, different bathroom. Granddaughter and dog across the hall. Daughter sleeping in the first-floor bedroom. New friend in the basement.

Not sleeping. Doing whatever she did. Going wherever

she went.

Normal.

"New friend."

Yes. A good friend. A wonderful friend. Taking care of her, Emmy, and Shelley. And Arnold.

The dog's small stroke or seizure or whatever it had been. One-time event. The drive to the vet. The money. The assurances about her Emmy not having COVID and her now getting better.

Her being "on the mend." Shelley liked that expression.

What a dear, little .. "she's a pistol." Debra could imagine her father saying that.

Her mind drifted.

Her mom's last words in the car, after the crash: "Please take care of my girls."

Her, Debra, so messed up back then.

Her, Emily, so young back then.

Debra gasped.

Her, little Shelley, at that time, existing only in the mind of God.

Now here. Across the hall. With Arnold.

Miriam, taking care of Mom's "girls.' Mom's *three* girls.

"Oh, Mom," Debra said. "Thank you. I'm so sorry I couldn't be the mother you were. I'm so sorry you didn't get to meet your great-granddaughter."

A thought: But maybe she had. Maybe their paths had crossed in heaven. After her death and before Shelley's birth. A happy thought.

Miriam there.

And Miriam here.

"I really don't want to screw this up." A prayer.

"And I really don't want to have to explain why I left little Emmy. Why my life got so screwed up. Why it went to hell."

Tears.

"And ... and ... and I really can't explain it. I really don't know, Lord. Little Jay."

Her stomach roiled. Saliva filled her mouth. She raced to the bathroom and threw up in the toilet, trying to be as quiet as possible. Hoping no one in the house heard her.

The monster under the bed.

49

Later that morning, late enough that it was light outside, Debra left her room and headed for the kitchen. Shelley, with Miriam's guiding hands, was pouring tea into a china cup on the table in front of where Debra usually sat.

"Do you like tea?" Shelley asked, her eyes not leaving the task at hand.

"I do."

"Good." Job done. Looking up. Smiling. "Mim said we could all have tea this morning."

"A wonderful idea." She looked at Miriam, whose face showed sympathy.

"And toast?" Shelley asked.

Debra thought for a moment. "Yes, please. One slice."

Shelley set the teapot down on a trivet and jumped to the toaster sitting on the counter.

"Dry, please," Debra added and the little girl stopped and turned. A piece of bread in each hand.

"That means nothing on it," Debra said. "No butter or jam or marmalade."

"Oh." Confused. Debra glad she hadn't ordered it "naked" as some patrons did at Wally's, the local diner.

"You made the tea," Miriam said. "Let me make the toast."

"Okay." Joining Debra at the table. "Is the tea good?"

"Perfect!"

A beaming face.

"You want toast?" Miriam asked Shelley.

"Yeah. One slice. Wet. Butter and jam."

"And ... ?" Miriam asked cupping her hand behind her ear."

Shelley, confused. "Oh. And a schmear."

"No, honey. I meant what's the magic word?"

A moment of reflection. Then: "Supercalifragilistic ... "

"Please," Debra prompted.

"Please."

After it was tea and one slice of dry toast for the ladies, tea and one slice of "wet" toast for the little girl, and two slices of buttered toast and a sniff at tea poured into a water bowl for the dog, Shelley asked: "So what are we going to do today?"

"What do you want to do?" Miriam said.

Obviously preplanned: "Tell stories."

"Like Goldilocks and the three ... " Debra began.

"No. About us!"

"Who goes first?" Miriam asked.

"Old people."

So Miriam told of "misplacing" Little Jay when he was twelve. Debra talked about getting her first dog, Spud. And then Shelley ... .

Both women knew something was up. Shelley had her head down. Saying nothing.

They waited.

"Something happened," she began and Debra and Miriam went on full alert.

They waited.

"When we left our 'partment and came up here."

They waited.

"There was a man who lived on the same floor and he saw us moving out and he said … something that sounded mean. Like he was glad we were going."

They waited.

"But we had to go. Mommy said we had to go and we'd find Grandma and she'd help us."

"What did the man say?" Miriam asked quietly.

"He called me something. A little pick something. Mommy said, 'Let's go' and we put more stuff in the car and we had just a little bit more to get out of the 'partment and we were going down the hall to get it and the man stuck his head out of his 'partment and he said, 'Bye bye, little … "

She stopped.

Miriam said, " 'Bye bye, little …' N-word."

"Yeah."

Hot anger flooded Debra.

"He was like Gramma," Shelley said. "I mean white. But not like Gramma! He was mean. He said things to Mommy that were mean, too, but I didn't know what they meant."

A pause.

"Am I a 'pick' whatever he said?"

"Pickaninny," Debra said. "That's a nasty and horrible word for a child that's your color."

Debra leaned in. "You know what else?"

Shelley shook her head.

"I want to punch him right in the nose."

The granddaughter smiled.

"And you know what else?" Miriam asked. She pushed back her chair and had Shelley come around the table and sit on her lap.

"You are a beautiful child of God," Miriam said, "who made you just the way you're supposed to be."

She wrapped her arms around her. Then whispered. "And that's what matters. That's why you matter. You are precious, precious, precious. And will be for all eternity."

The women could see the little girl relaxing. Then: "Right in the nose, Gramma?"

50

The following mid-afternoon. Debra in the bedroom visiting with Emily. The conversation easy, relaxed. Miriam and Shelley taking Arnold for a walk in a light mist.

Then:

The sound of the front door opening and an eighty-pound dog bounding into the bedroom and leaping up on the bed.

A wet eighty-pound dog.

Standing. Shaking himself as dry as possible.

Mother and daughter yelping and laughing.

A granddaughter, at the doorway, joining in.

A granddaughter wearing a dark brown scarf.

Miriam's scarf. Arranged as Miriam had had it on the day Debra had beaned her with the bag.

And Debra knew something was up.

"Mim said she had to go see some other friends," Shelley said. "She called them 'dear ones.'"

"She got down on one knee like this ... " Shelley demonstrated. " ... and gave Arnold a hug and he smelled the top of her head and both of them laughed."

Debra and Emily said nothing. Then Shelley to Emily: "Did you know Arnold can laugh?" and the moms nodded.

"Then she put her scarf on me like this and gave me a hug and said she would always be here and here." Shelley tapped her forehead and her chest.

"And then she walked around the corner where the new house is."

She paused.

"And one more thing."

The women waited.

Shelley stood up and tapped her mother and grandmother on the forehead and on the chest.

"She said she'll always be here and here with you, too."

Tears spilled down Debra's cheeks.

"And then she came back from around the corner and she waved and yelled, 'Always!'"

"Then disappeared around the corner," Debra whispered.

"Yeah."

51

One week later a padded manila envelope showed up in the mail. From: A post office box somewhere in Louisiana. To: Shelley Patrick and Debra Patrick.

With a little effort and her grandmother's encouragement, Shelley was able to tear it open and take a peek. Debra held out cupped hands and Shelley dumped the contents into them.

Two slender, stainless steel, chain link necklaces. One sheet of paper missing the hands and drifting to the floor.

Shelley easily bent over and picked it up. "French." Pointing to the letterhead: *Couvent de Notre Dame du Diamant Noir.* Recognizing the language but unable to read it, just as her ability to read English was limited.

She plucked one of necklaces out of Debra's hands and looked at the stainless steel disk attached to it. A little smaller than a quarter. "Mim," she said, showing Debra the image of the face. "What's it say?"

Debra looked, nodded, and read the words curving over the top of Miriam's head: "Blessed Loving Mother."

Then: A memory, an echo, from when Miriam had been there only a short while. "You deserve a medal." But only

one. Wanting two would be … what word had she used? —
unseemly.

"Is this a word?" Shelley asked, looking at the back of the
medal.

An initialism, an abbreviation formed from initial letters.

Blessed Loving Mother.

Black Lives Matter.

BLM.

EPILOGUE
Summer 2050

This isn't the first book I've attempted to write. It *is* the first one I've completed. Or almost completed. I know I have to clear up some things. Fill in some blanks.

To borrow a term from Ricky Ricardo scolding Lucy (from about a century ago): I got some 'splainin' to do.

I've had a lot of free time for writing over the past six weeks. Or, better put, down time. And more weeks yet to come.

That's because of the twins I'm carrying, two daughters yet to come. Itty-bitty girls who have yet to make their appearance, except on ultrasounds.

There have been some issues with the pregnancy, nothing too serious my ob-gyn assures me, that have sent me to bed. Safe over sorry.

Fine with me.

So … here's a little bit of what's gone on since Mim waved goodbye.

(And it's in a really jumbled order. I have no idea of how to make it chronologically coherent when one event smears into another. Plus, I'm sure I'll write them as they occur to me. Maybe someday I'll straighten all this out. I don't see that happening until my girls are grown up. Plus a few years.)

* * *

At some point in the last thirty years I switched from "Shelley" to "Rochelle." I suppose what I thought was a perfect name for an almost-five-year-old wasn't as pleasing for a young woman of twenty or so.

I like that I was named for my great-grandmother. I like the idea of one of my daughters being named Debra and the other named Miriam.

Antonio, my husband of four years, is a very agreeable fellow. "Deb" and "Mim" are fine. And the girls' middle names will be his *abuelas'* names: Maria and Anna.

Anyway, being stuck in bed had me thinking about when I was a little girl and remembering my meeting "Gramma Debby" and her pal, " Mim."

Needless to say, stuff was going on from the eve of Mim's appearance to the day of her moving on that I knew nothing about. Not then and not later, until Gramma told me more about it and Mom added to it after Gramma died in 2029 at the age of seventy-four.

* * *

I think I remember more about the Old World because Mom packed up our lives and drove north. A lot of people my age—and even a little older—have no memories of that time. Of those years before the COVID-19 pandemic and of the pandemic itself.

And, of course, people younger than I am know only the New World.

I suspect it was that way for people who were old enough to remember the time before World War II and could compare it to the period following it. There was no going back to how it had been before 1939 and the Nazis invading Poland. Or, for Americans, before 1941and the bombing of Pearl Harbor.

After the war, and after the pandemic, what had been

normal was gone. Replaced by what some twenty-first-century old-timers still call the "new normal."

* * *

I spent today reading what I had written—and going to the bathroom, "That's not a trampoline, ladies, that's my bladder"—and I see that there are a lot of half-told stories. An item mentioned without further explanation.

Like Grandpa Mike's death. Or Dad's getting deported. Or Gramma leaving her little family when she was in her thirties. And more!

If I were a better writer, if I were a "real writer" at all, I would know how to seamlessly fold that information into the main narrative. (That sounds impressive, coming from a social worker.)

But I'm not. And I don't.

So here's a bit more of what I found out from Gramma and Mom. (And a bit more about me.)

I am so, so glad I bugged Gramma to tell me these stories. And for the ones she shared without my asking. Some very hard ones.

And I am so, so glad that Mom filled in some blanks and is still around to answer my questions now.

* * *

Arnold, who in my early memory was bigger than a horse and really could talk, passed away in his sleep in 2025. Mom and Gramma had warned me it was coming.

The three of us and Dad (more on that in a bit) buried him in the back yard—and, oh, how I cried. We planted a little dogwood tree sapling at the head of the plot. It took several years before it blossomed and I was thrilled to see they weren't white petals but pink!

Still my favorite color.

* * *

Grandpa Mike had lived on the other side of the country. I never met him and he died when I was three so I wasn't much affected by his death. What I do, sort of, remember, is

Dad (*Mon père*) being home with me and Mom being gone.

She flew back to be with Grandpa when he died and stayed through the funeral and burial. Not much longer after that Dad was scooped up by the Feds, held for a short time, and then sent back to Haiti. He had overstayed his (legal) welcome and my parents weren't married. Apparently, having an American child didn't cut it during that period. Or some such.

Shortly after that Mom lost her job, the bills piled up, we got evicted, and Gramma was our only hope. (Amazing how little a child knows about what's really going on.)

It was a few years before all of Dad's paperwork would be sorted out and he could join us in Black Diamond. (I remember *that* day!)

Oh. More on Mom and Dad. Mom majored in French and education in college and served in the Peace Corps in Haiti after graduation. There she met guess who? He came to the States and didn't leave until he was dragged out.

At that time Mom, who had been teaching French in a private school that went belly up, had a minimum-wage, no-future job. Where she was laid off. So … after a bit: to the north.

* * *

I was fourteen when Gramma died (her death *really* affected me). While Grandpa had had no "earthly goods" to leave to Mom, Gramma had the house, its contents, and a tidy little nest egg.

The money went to Mom and Dad, the house and its contents to me. Under Mom's guardianship until I was eighteen.

So when I entered Black Diamond High School (Class of 2033) I was a homeowner.

I still live here, with my dear Antonio and our two in-process daughters. All four of us will use the big bedroom on the first floor until the girls are old enough to move upstairs.

I suspect they'll want to be in the same bedroom until they decide they each want one their own.

After Dad rejoined us, he and a neighbor (in the monstrosity house) helped Dad enlarge the bedroom in the basement. Mom and Dad lived there. Gramma was back in her room. And Arnold and I were upstairs.

I miss those days.

Now my folks own a condo in Buckeye, Arizona, but come north often. (In the summer.) I assume they'll visit even more frequently after The Big Day.

Dad and Antonio have taught Mom and me a lot of about family, family, family!

It's wonderful. (This whispered: Most of the time.)

* * *

In 2020, Mom had had just enough money for gas to get us up to Gramma's. They hadn't been in contact for a long, long time.

Gramma had disappeared and there was no trace of "Debra Therese Patrick" on the Internet. Mom had searched and searched as her flu/cold got worse and worse. And the money ran out.

For some reason ("some reason"), she gave St. Anthony the boot. He wasn't getting the job done. (Patron saint of finding lost items, ha!)

Instead, and she still gets this look in her eyes when she repeats the story now, Mom said a Hail Mary. First time in many, many years but still remembered word-for-word. Still there, buried in her memory. Her heart. Still able to call it up and say it with great passion.

That Mim is a sneaky one.

Boom. On the net. An address. Gramma Debby's. And away we went, that very day. Arriving just before Mom passed out and with just enough gas in the tank for Mim's friends to get "the donkey" moved to a spot in front of Gramma's house.

There is a story in the Bible (Numbers 22:21-34) about a

donkey and an angel but I don't know if it was one of the guys who moved Mom's car.

* * *

About the medals. I'm wearing mine now and Gramma's is in my top dresser drawer. Someday I'll give them to the girls.

Their lives matter.

Mim's scarf is in the same drawer. Down the road, I'll cut it in two (pinking shears!) and hem each half.

The piece of paper, the letter, that came with the medals is tucked away there, too. It's from a convent in Diamant Noir, Louisiana. That's French for Black Diamond.

Our Black Diamond, in Washington state, got its name because of the coals mines that used to be worked here. Louisiana had, has, a town named Diamond. Or Diamant. It's a Cajun area so French is still common.

Some long, hard years after the Civil War, freed slaves had saved enough to pool their money and buy some "worthless" land not far from there. It became known as "Black Diamond."

One of those founders was only four when she was freed. Twenty years later she joined together with other women and they began (really she began) The Sisters of the Blessed Loving Mother. Their habit was (is) light brown with a darker brown veil.

The veils, scarves really, were originally made from empty feed sacks.

The foundress' religious name was Sister Mary Margaret. Her birth name was Monica Faudree. She kept a journal that tells of the Blessed Mother visiting her over a period of two months just before the start of the twentieth century.

Mim!

As has happened in other times and places, Mim told the visionary to have a medal struck with her image and said what she wanted printed on it, front and back.

Sister Mary Margaret passed away in 1949. At the

beginning of the twenty-first century, she was on track to being canonized and the order (and donors/benefactors) had finally had the medals made.

Gramma's and my name were found on a list Sister had written by hand. The address, too. Long before we were born or our house had been built.

Oh, that Mim!

* * *

The "monstrosity house" was completed in late summer and the multigenerational family that moved in included a girl who was five. Teresa.

We would sit in little plastic chairs on opposite sides of the chain link fence separating the lots. Each of us in itty-bitty pink facemasks. (Gramma and I had made them. Mostly Gramma.) At that point not as necessary but fun.

We'd just jabber away and Arnold would interrupt every once in a while to let us know there was a squirrel nearby. And he'd bark "hello" and jump up on the fence if Teresa's brother came out on their porch. Three years older than us.

Antonio.

Yeah.

Teresa and I went through high school together. She became a doctor. I'm a social worker (therapist/counselor).

And we're sisters-in-law!

* * *

I know Gramma influenced my career choice. Or the career that chose me.

Gramma started going to therapy after Mim left us. I knew nothing of this until I was in my early teens. Then—I remember it clearly—one day she sat me down at the kitchen table and told me what had happened to her as a teen.

In her light blue prom dress.

After the dance, her date—a "nice boy" two years older than she was—sexually assaulted her. She told no one. Assumed it was all her fault.

He had nothing more to do with her.

Her grades and behavior plummeted the next school year. She got it together enough to try college, soon dropped out, moved out, and began working full time at a dead-end job.

She met Grandpa, who really was a nice boy, got married, had Mom, and—again—held it together for a while. Then …

Drinking, drugs, sleeping around.

Doing her best to cope. Forget. Deal with.

Big time depression. Big time pain.

Doing her best not to kill herself.

She ran away. That was how she looked at it for most of her life.

She *survived.* She got a glimmer of that truth, that accomplishment, after—during—her ongoing therapy.

One of her greatest fears much later in life was that the same thing would happen to me.

There was a lot more information, help, and understanding in the 2020s compared to the 1970s.

But still.

I think of the 2060s, when my little ones will be in their teens.

I'm sure some young women and young men, some girls and boys, will be hurt that way.

Just as I'm sure, I know, racism hasn't ended.

And that Mim will "take care of *my* girls."

As we sat at that kitchen table, Gramma said all those feelings and memories were stirred up after Mom and I arrived. Not that the stirring was our fault. And, she said time and again, it was good that she dealt with it.

"Kicked its ass," in her words. As much as possible, stomped "the monster under the bed."

Came to understand why—like that blue, lightly woven piece of fabric out of which I had pulled one thread—there was a gap, things missing and not understood, in her life.

And, to some degree, always would be.

But she came to know a peace that had been gone since before that prom night.

I want to help others like others helped Gramma Debby.

* * *

Oh. About the COVID 19 virus. I'm not sure of the chronology of all that. What happened when. Globally, and in our little world. Masks and quarantines and social distancing and vaccines and all the rest.

* * *

I wish I had a photo of Mim. That all of us were in the one picture she took. Mom was too pooped, I was a kid, and Gramma had ... limited ... smart-phone skills. Yes, they were considered "smart" phones. ("What's a phone, Mom?" my kids will ask me. Smart-alecks.)

The image on the medal, and paintings and illustrations of "Our Lady of Black Diamond," are very accurate.

I do wish I had a recording of her laugh-snort.

Gramma, Mom, and I never went public about our time with her. Not that we agreed to keep mum on Mim, we just never did. We kept her, that time, those events, to ourselves. Mom told Dad. I've told Antonio. But that was all, till now.

I wrote this for my girls so that, someday they'll know, too. I want them to know about her. I want them to know *her*.

* * *

After that afternoon when she waved goodbye and walked around the corner, I never saw Mim again.

Since then, she's always been with me and, I know, always will be.

ABOUT THE AUTHOR

Bill Dodds has been writing professionally since the days of carbon paper. He's the author of more than forty books, including:

Fiction

Golden

My Great-grandfather Turns 12 Today (for kids)

The World's Funniest Atheist

Mildred Nudge: A Widower's Tale

Pope Bob

Nonfiction

On Your Pilgrimage Called Grief:
A Guide for Widows and Widowers

How to Write Your Novel in Nine Weeks

What You Don't Know About Retirement (humor)

What You Don't Know About Turning 40 (humor)

Learn more at BillDodds.com
Contact Bill at wfdodds@gmail.com

20210704

IF YOU WANT TO SAY
HELLO TO MIM

Hail Mary, full of grace,
the Lord is with you.
Blessed are you among women
and blessed is the fruit of your womb, Jesus.

Holy Mary, Mother of God,
pray for us sinners now
and at the hour of our death.
Amen.

Our Lady of
(wherever you, dear reader, are right now),
pray for us.

www.ingramcontent.com/pod-product-compliance
Lightning Source LLC
Chambersburg PA
CBHW050950120626
46552CB00001B/475